Pretty Little Monster

by Molly Pyne

ISBN-13: 979-8-89901-995-1

This book is dedicated to my two beautiful daughters, Charlotte and Ella. You are my heart, my inspiration, and the reason I strive to be better every day.

Your strength, humor, and resilience continue to amaze me. I am so proud of the incredible people you are becoming. I love you both more than anything in this world, and this one is for you.

Love forever and always,
Mommy

Molly Pyne

1

The air hung thick with the scent of lilies and something else, something metallic and faintly sweet, that clung to the back of my throat like a phantom kiss. Polished mahogany and cold, sterile perfection marked his office, reflecting the man himself: Arthur Blackwood, CEO of Blackwood Industries. This titan of industry built his empire on the backs of others, treating compassion as a weakness and empathy as a liability. He was my first. My masterpiece.

I'd studied him for months, a predator observing its prey. I devoured news articles, social media posts, anything that offered a glimpse into his meticulously crafted persona. I learned his routines, his habits, his vulnerabilities. He was predictable, tragically so. His arrogance, his unshakeable belief in his own invincibility, became his undoing.

The security system was a joke, a testament to his misplaced confidence. I bypassed it with the ease of someone unlocking a child's toy box. I knew the exact time he would be alone, the precise moment when his defenses were at their lowest. It wasn't brute force that brought him down; it was intellect, strategy, a meticulous dance of manipulation.

Blackwood's routine was predictable, almost mechanical. Tuesday evenings, invariably, he'd have a late dinner at his club, returning around 10:30 PM. His security system, while sophisticated, relied on motion sensors, easily bypassed with a little finesse.

I gained access through a cleverly placed EMP burst, disrupting the security system for a critical window. It was a calculated risk, but the potential reward outweighed the slight probability of detection. The disruption was brief, timed precisely to coincide with Blackwood's approach to his home, ensuring no lasting damage or suspicion. The house presented a minor obstacle itself. Standard security measures secured the perimeter, and CCTV cameras were in place. But again, the predictability proved useful.

I noted the precise timing of his nightly rounds, and the areas not covered by cameras. I used a small drone equipped with thermal imaging to scan the house's interior. Locating his study was trivial; his lifestyle had made that obvious. The drone hovered just beneath the ceiling's threshold, avoiding the detection zones.

The study itself was a marvel of organization—a chaotic order, in a way, a reflection of the man himself. The office was a treasure trove of information. His digital security, however, was surprisingly robust. Luckily, I had expected this. I'd planted a tiny key-logger several weeks ago during a seemingly innocuous social event—a simple pretext for getting close and planting the device unnoticed. I retrieved the data—crucial financial records, correspondence detailing his illegal activities—all neatly packaged and ready to be transferred offsite.

The thrill of the hunt was intoxicating, a heady cocktail of adrenaline and anticipation. Each carefully calculated step, each silent movement, felt like a brush against the edge of oblivion. The power, the control, was absolute. It was a game, yes, but a game with terrifyingly high stakes. And I was winning.

The moment I entered his office, the air crackled with unspoken tension. Engrossed in a document, he hunched over his desk, oblivious to my presence. The shadows played across his face, transforming his features into something almost grotesque, a caricature of his own self-importance. I approached him slowly, savoring the moment, feeling the shift in the atmosphere, a silent acknowledgment of the inevitable.

There was no struggle, no scream. Just the soft thud of his body hitting the plush carpet, the muffled gasp escaping his lips before the darkness claimed him from one swift jab of my syringe filled with a lethal amount of air. It was immediate, efficient, almost clinical. I wouldn't say it was beautiful, not in the traditional sense. But there was a certain elegance in its precision, a disturbing symmetry in the way everything fell into place.

The ritual was the most important part. It was the culmination of the hunt, the act of claiming my trophy. From each victim, I take something small, something that represents their essence, their power, their very being. From Blackwood, it was a cufflink, an obsidian stone carved into the shape of a raven with a black diamond replacing its eye. A fitting symbol for a man who shrouded himself in darkness, who preyed on the unsuspecting.

The extraction was quick and clean. I was already gone before the house's security system fully rebooted. There was a silence, broken only by the rhythmic tick of the clock.

As I held the obsidian raven in my hand, a strange sense of satisfaction washed over me. It wasn't a feeling of blood-lust, not exactly. It was more… a sense of balance restored. A twisted sense of justice, perhaps. He was a man who had caused immeasurable suffering, who had trampled on others without a second thought. I was merely redistributing the wealth, so to speak, evening the score. It was a dark, disturbing justification, I know, but it was the only one that made sense to me. The only one that silenced the whispers in the back of my mind.

The raven felt cold against my skin, smooth and strangely comforting. As I held it, I felt a strange power surge through me, a potent energy I couldn't quite explain. It wasn't a physical sensation, more of a feeling of… absorption, like I was becoming part of him, inheriting his essence. Was it just a psychological effect? Perhaps. Or perhaps there was something more to it. Perhaps something dark and ancient, something beyond the comprehension of mere mortals.

The police arrived hours later, their presence a discordant note in the symphony of my triumph. Detective Michael Stone, a man whose eyes held the weight of a thousand unsolved cases, was the lead investigator. His gaze, sharp and incisive, felt like a physical blow. He proved a worthy adversary, a man not easily manipulated. But even he, with his years of experience, would find himself ensnared in my web of carefully constructed illusions.

The media frenzy that followed was a predictable, yet satisfying, spectacle. News reports detailed the ruthless CEO's untimely and unsolved murder. The public, ravenous for details, hung onto every scrap of information, their fascination mirroring my own. Their morbid curiosity was a perverse validation, a silent acknowledgment of my success.

I surveyed the room: the victim lay still, the scene carefully staged to appear as a natural death. I used gloves and a cleaning solution to eliminate any fingerprints from surfaces. Any loose strands of hair or fabric that may have been disturbed were removed. The entry point showed no signs of forced entry. I even took the extra step of wiping down the window I entered through. Finally, I changed my clothes, disposed of the gloves and cleaning materials in separate, secure locations. I left, meticulously erasing any trace of my presence.

The police would find nothing. My plan's elegant simplicity would leave them baffled and frustrate their efforts. They would chase shadows, following false leads, while I watched, unseen, from the periphery, relishing their frustration.

But Stone was different. He had a way of seeing beneath the surface, a capacity to decipher the unspoken, to sense the subtle nuances that others missed. His obsession would grow, mirroring my own, becoming an inextricable part of this twisted game. He wouldn't just be investigating a murder; he would embark on a descent into the labyrinth of my mind, a journey that would challenge his perceptions and ultimately unravel his sanity.

He wouldn't find me easily. I had already moved on to my next target, another member of society's elite, another individual whose wealth and power masked a darkness far deeper than their own. The hunt had only just begun. The game, my game, was far from over. And with each successful kill, with each carefully selected trophy, my power would only grow, my influence expanding like a malignant tumor in the heart of society. The obsidian raven, a small, perfectly crafted symbol, was only the beginning. The collection had begun, and the world would soon tremble under the weight of my ambition.

I recognized the irony. They mourned Blackwood, a man who had shown no mercy, no compassion. They bemoaned the loss of a powerful executive, a pillar of the community. But I saw something else. I saw the balance restored, the scales of justice, however twisted, righted. And as I watched Stone's investigation unfold, his growing obsession feeding my own, I couldn't help but feel a twisted sense of triumph. This was only the first act. The curtain had risen, and the show was about to begin. With the stage set, I took center stage. The audience, willingly or not, became captivated. And my next performance promised to be even more spectacular.

2

They call it justice. The newspapers, the talking heads on television, the whispering voices in the crowded streets—they all clamor for justice, yet they cannot see it when it stares them in the face. Or perhaps they see it, but they refuse to acknowledge it, blinded by their own self-righteous indignation. They demand retribution for the sins of others, yet they ignore the sins within their own gilded cages. They cling to their morality, their carefully constructed narratives, while the world crumbles around them, a monument to hypocrisy and greed.

I am the balance. I am the silent hand that redistributes the wealth, the unseen force that corrects the inequities of this rotten system. They see a monster, a killer, a fiend. All they see is blood, violence, and grotesque rituals. They cannot see the meticulously crafted plan, the strategic precision, the underlying philosophy. They see the chaos, but not the order that precedes it, the equilibrium I strive to create in a world desperately in need of it.

My victims are not random. I choose each one carefully; they are studies in privilege and corruption. Their wealth, their influence, their absolute disregard for the suffering of others — these are the criteria I used to judge them. They are the architects of societal decay, the ones who profit from the misery of the masses. They live in their ivory towers, oblivious to the consequences of their actions, cocooned in a world of luxury and indifference.

I dismantle their carefully constructed facades. I expose their vulnerabilities, their hidden depravities. I strip them bare, revealing the rot beneath the polished surface. And in doing so, I restore a semblance of order, a fragile balance in a world teetering on the brink of collapse. This is not revenge; it's a surgical strike against the heart of injustice. It's a necessary evil, a bitter pill they must swallow to purge their system of its inherent corruption.

The rituals are not mere theatrics. They are a symbolic dismantling of their power, a ceremonial stripping away of their arrogance. The trophies I take—a lock of hair, a precious ring, a meticulously crafted cufflink—are not mementos of violence but representations of their essence, their power, the influence they wielded over the lives of others. I absorb their energy, their strength, their very being, incorporating them into myself, making their power my own.

Some might call it cannibalism, a grotesque act of appropriation. Perhaps they are right. But they cannot see the purpose, the meaning behind the ritual. It's not about consuming flesh and blood, it's about absorbing their very being. It's about transforming their power into something new, something more potent, something that can create a better world, a world free from the constraints of their greed and corruption.

Do I feel remorse? Do I feel guilt? These are emotions reserved for the weak, for those who are incapable of seeing the bigger picture, for those who cannot comprehend the necessity of sacrifice. I am not weak. I am a force of nature, a necessary evil, a cleansing fire that purifies the corruption and restores balance to the scales of justice.

And you… you are my confidante, my silent partner in this endeavor. You read my words; you absorb my story, and you remain silent. As we both know, you are complicit. You find yourself drawn to my narrative, captivated by my methods, and yet you remain silent. My dear reader, you are not innocent. You have become part of this game, this twisted dance of morality and chaos. I have entangled you in my web of lies, and you cannot escape.

The game continues. The next target has been chosen. Another paragon of virtue, another pillar of society, another figure who hides their depravity beneath a veneer of respectability. I have studied them, observed them, anticipated their moves. I know their routines, their vulnerabilities, their deepest secrets. Soon, I will claim another trophy and another soul for myself.

The police, led by that perpetually frustrated Detective Stone, continue their futile pursuit. Chasing shadows and following dead ends, their investigations take them further and further from the truth. Their own preconceived notions blind them with their rigid adherence to outdated procedures, their refusal to see the bigger picture. They are pawns in my game, unwitting participants in a drama they cannot comprehend.

But they are not my primary concern. My focus is on the game itself, the intricate dance of manipulation and deception. The thrill of the hunt, the exquisite pleasure of outsmarting them, of leaving no trace, of remaining unseen, unheard, untouchable—this is the true reward. It is a symphony of chaos and control, a meticulously crafted masterpiece of psychological warfare.

And you, my silent accomplice, my trusted confidante, you are the audience to this grand spectacle. You are a witness to my triumph, a silent observer of my actions. Silently, you watch me dismantle the pillars of society, one by one, captivated by my audacity, skill, and unwavering resolve. You are a part of this, whether or not you like it. You are complicit in this, and utterly captivated by my actions.

So let the game continue. Let the hunt begin. My plan's inevitable unfolding will make the world tremble. Let the chaos ensue. Restore the balance. Let the collection grow.

Because in the end, it's not about the blood, not about the violence, not about the trophies. It's about the game. It's about the power. It's about the control. The exquisite, intoxicating thrill of watching the world burn is mine alone, as I orchestrated its destruction and twisted rebirth. And you, my dear reader, are watching it all unfold along with me. The curtain has risen; the stage has been set, and the performance has just begun. You are a participant. Whether or not you like it. The final curtain will fall sooner than you think. And when it does, I wonder what you'll do.

3

The rain pounded against the corrugated iron roof of the precinct, a relentless percussion mirroring the relentless ache in Detective Michael Stone's skull. He swirled the lukewarm coffee in his mug, the bitter taste doing little to ease the gnawing emptiness inside him. Five years. Five years since the Mallory case, five years since the face of a young girl, her eyes wide with terror, had haunted his dreams. Five years since he'd failed.

The Mallory case file, thick with dust and unopened for years, detailed the events of a cold autumn evening. Eight-year-old Mallory Thompson was last seen playing near her home, a small cottage at the edge of Natolatta Forest. Her disappearance triggered a large-scale search, but only yielded her bright yellow raincoat, found snagged on a low-hanging branch deep within the woods.

Three days later, a local hunter discovered Mallory's body near a shallow stream. Her location was over a mile from her home, suggesting someone had carried her. The forensic report detailed blunt force trauma to the head, consistent with a heavy, possibly blunt object. There were no signs of sexual assault. The time of death was placed within hours of her disappearance. Despite extensively questioning neighbors and the surrounding community, investigators found no witnesses.

Police investigated various suspects, including known offenders in the area, but no conclusive evidence emerged. Investigators never found a murder weapon. The investigation eventually stalled, the lack of concrete evidence halting any meaningful leads.

The case remained open, yet unsolved, a cold stain on the town's history. Mallory's small grave, marked by a simple headstone, lay quietly amidst the autumn leaves, a silent testament to a life cut tragically short. The yellow raincoat, now a key piece of evidence, sat in the evidence locker, folded neatly, a haunting reminder of the unanswered questions surrounding the Mallory case.

This case… this new one… it was different, yet disturbingly familiar. The victims, all wealthy, all influential, all seemingly unconnected except for one horrifying detail: a missing artifact, something small, something precious, something symbolic. A lock of platinum blonde hair from the esteemed philanthropist, Lady Beatrice Worthington. A diamond raven cufflink from the ruthless CEO, Arthur Blackwood. A ruby pendant, intricately carved, from the reclusive art collector, Alistair Finch. The police had labeled it 'The Collector's Eye', a morbid joke that gnawed at Stone's already frayed nerves. This case… this new one… it was different, yet disturbingly familiar.

He slammed the mug down; the clatter echoing in the near-empty office. His colleagues, weary from the relentless pressure, had dispersed, leaving him alone to wrestle with the ever-deepening mystery. The killer was a ghost, a phantom weaving a tapestry of elaborate deception. The killer meticulously staged the crime scenes, almost theatrical in their precision. There was no forced entry, no sign of struggle, no witnesses. It was as if the victims had willingly surrendered their lives, their possessions, their very essence. And that was what truly unnerved him.

Stone ran a hand through his thinning hair, the gesture revealing the strain etched into his face. He was a man carved by grief and shadowed by failure, his sharp eyes perpetually searching for a pattern that wouldn't appear. The Mallory case was a scar he carried with him, an open wound that bled into every investigation, a relentless whisper of inadequacy in the back of his mind. The thought of failing again, of another innocent life lost to a killer he couldn't catch, was a weight heavy enough to crush him.

The profiler, Dr. Emily Carter, had suggested a female perpetrator, a sophisticated, highly intelligent individual with a deep understanding of human psychology. But her profile felt too… neat, too easily categorized. Stone suspected a deeper, more disturbing motivation than simple thrill-seeking or monetary gain. He saw chilling intelligence at play, a carefully orchestrated dance of death. The killer wasn't just killing; they were playing a game, and Stone was a reluctant participant.

He picked up the file, the thin paper crinkling beneath his touch. Each victim's life story was a testament to privilege and excess. Lady Beatrice, with her lavish charity galas and suspiciously gained fortune. Blackwood, his ruthless business tactics and unwavering ambition. Finch, his hoard of priceless artifacts and rumored involvement in illegal antiquities dealing. They were not saints; they were flawed, yes, but they weren't murderers. Or were they? The killer's narrative, discovered in a cryptic message left at each scene, painted a disturbingly persuasive picture of societal imbalance.

The message was a taunt, a perverse justification for their actions. It spoke of a balance being restored, of the rich being held accountable, of a 'cleansing' necessary to purify a corrupt world. Stone initially dismissed it as the ramblings of a deranged mind, but the more he delved into the victims' backgrounds, the more uneasy the message became. It was a mirror reflecting the dark underbelly of their lives, the secrets they had so carefully guarded. The killer knew them intimately, understood their weaknesses, their vulnerabilities, their deepest fears.

Stone's obsession deepened with each passing day. He pored over the victims' financial records, social media activity, even their personal journals—a transgression he knew was against procedure, a violation of privacy, but he couldn't stop himself. The killer's psychological manipulation was masterful. It was as if they were guiding him, feeding him information, leading him down a carefully laid path. The more he investigated, the further he seemed to get from the truth. Deception trapped him in a maze, a labyrinth of carefully constructed lies. His frustration simmered, building into a rage that threatened to consume him.

The rain continued to downpour in the city, reflecting the chaos and despair that Stone felt churning inside him. He rubbed his tired eyes, the city lights blurring into a hazy reflection of his own clouded thoughts. Heavy with the city's burden, its unsolved mysteries, and his own failures, he felt crushed. He was drowning in this case, consumed by it, obsessed by it.

He looked at the photograph of Lady Beatrice; her smile strained, her eyes reflecting a chilling emptiness. The killer had taken something more than just a lock of hair; they had taken a piece of her soul, a fragment of her very being. He felt a strange kinship with the victims now, a shared vulnerability, a recognition of the unseen dangers lurking beneath the surface of their apparently perfect lives. He saw the carefully constructed façades, the hidden vulnerabilities, the rot beneath the polished surface. The killer's justification, although twisted and monstrous, resonated on a primal level. They had exposed the hypocrisy, the greed, the arrogance.

The phone rang, jarring him from his reverie. It was Carter. "Stone," her voice was sharp, efficient, "We have another one. Baroness Anya Petrova. Same MO. Same message. Only this time… the trophy was… different."

Stone felt a chill crawl down his spine. He hadn't yet realized the pattern in the trophies. Until now. It wasn't about the object itself. It was about the symbolism. The sequence. This wasn't random. This was a meticulously planned narrative, a twisted story only the killer could understand. And Stone was now a character in that story, whether or not he liked it.

The game, it seemed, was far from over. In fact, it was only just the beginning. He knew, with an icy certainty, that the next victim was closer than he thought. He felt certain the killer would fully reveal themselves and unveil the last piece of their carefully crafted puzzle; it was only a matter of time. The last act of this twisted drama was about to begin, and Stone, despite himself, found himself drawn to the edge of the precipice, ready to stare into the abyss. He was caught. Entangled. Complicit. And terrified. The rain continued to fall, washing away the dirt and grime of the city, but leaving the stain of dread firmly imprinted on Stone's weary soul.

4

The ruby pendant, nestled in its velvet-lined box, pulsed with a faint, inner light. I held it to my palm, feeling the warmth seep into my skin, a phantom heat that lingered even after I set it down. Alistair Finch, the reclusive collector, hadn't merely possessed it; he'd inhabited it. The crimson depths of the gemstone showed his obsession, avarice, and very essence, a testament to his life's singular focus. And now it was mine.

Each acquisition was a conquest, not merely a theft. It wasn't about the monetary value—although Finch's collection was worth a king's ransom. It was about the soul, the essence, the concentrated power of a life lived to the extreme. I wasn't just stealing; I was absorbing. The lock of platinum blonde hair from Lady Beatrice, shimmering like spun moonlight, was the arrogance of untold wealth, the effortless charm that masked a heart of cold calculation. The black diamond cufflink from Blackwood, sharp and glittering, was the ruthless ambition, the cutthroat determination that had propelled him to the pinnacle of the corporate ladder.

These weren't random acts of violence. This wasn't about blood, though there was plenty of that. It was about ritual. A meticulous, carefully orchestrated dance designed to extract the very essence of their being, to distill their power and absorb it into my own. It was a transference, a dark communion. I studied them, learned their patterns, their fears, their weaknesses. I became them, in a sense, inhabiting their skin, walking in their gilded cages before dismantling their carefully constructed worlds. It was a performance, a theatrical display of justice, a reclamation of what they had stolen from the world.

The blood, of course, was essential. The life force, the vitality. But it wasn't the primary purpose. The blood was merely the medium, the conduit through which I accessed the true prize—the essence of their being captured and contained within their prized possessions. The ritual was precise. A single, clean incision, never messy or brutal, a surgical strike that prioritized efficiency and symbolism. I didn't want to desecrate the body; I wanted to extract the essence, to leave the physical form intact, a husk emptied of its significance.

I prefer the darkness, the quiet hum of the night. The city sleeps, oblivious to the intricate dance of death being performed in its shadowed corners. But sometimes, I linger just to watch the dawn break, the city awakening to a new day, unaware of the subtle shifts in the balance of power. I am a ghost, a shadow, a phantom that moves unseen, unheard, leaving behind only a faint trace, a subtle alteration in the fabric of reality. The world doesn't know what it's lost. It doesn't even realize it's missing anything. Yet.

Each death was a painstaking process, both mentally and physically. The planning, the research, the anticipation—it was almost… exhilarating. It's intoxicating: the thrill of the chase, the satisfaction of the hunt, the precise execution of the plan. The meticulously curated crime scenes were not for show; they were part of the ritual. They were a message, a dark sonnet composed of blood and symbolism. A challenge. A game.

The message left at each scene—a taunting reminder of

my presence, my power. A cryptic message composed of symbols, metaphors, and allusions, only I could understand. I did not intend it for the police. For those I targeted. It was a warning, a prophecy of their impending doom. It was a perverse acknowledgment of their culpability. They were not victims; they were players in a game of their own making, oblivious pawns in a drama they had orchestrated themselves.

The Baroness… Anya Petrova. Her trophy was different. A small, intricately carved ivory figurine. Not a diamond, not a gemstone, not hair. A figurine. It was subtle, almost hidden, yet it resonated with an unsettling power. Her face serene and almost ethereal, the depiction showed a woman whose eyes held a cold, knowing glint. It was chillingly familiar.

The significance of the figurine became clear only after the acquisition. It wasn't a random choice. That marked the end of the sequence. It wasn't about wealth, or power, or influence; it was about beauty, about perfection, about the unattainable ideal. Petrov's trophy represents all that they had sought after and failed to achieve, a pointed reflection of their empty pursuits. It's not about vengeance, it's about exposing the flaws, the hypocrisy, the lies. The imbalance.

The sequence wasn't merely chronological; it was symbolic. It was a narrative, a twisted parable played out in the lives and deaths of the privileged few. The hair, the cufflink, the ruby, and finally, the figurine. Four stages of the human condition. Arrogance, ambition, avarice, and ultimately, the desperate pursuit of the unattainable ideal of beauty and perfection. The pursuit of that which cannot be obtained. It highlights their futility and underscores the inherent flaws in their existence.

The figurine holds a deeper significance. It mirrors my victims' vain hopes for perfection; serving as a reminder, a chilling testament to their shallowness, their arrogance, their desperate attempts to fill the void within their opulent existence. It symbolized the hollowness at the heart of their lives. It is a representation of the empty pursuit of false ideals. And it is mine.

The police, Detective Stone, he's relentless, isn't he? He's close. He sees the patterns, the symbolism, the narrative. He almost understands. Almost. He's a pawn in the game. A reluctant participant in my carefully orchestrated drama; a catalyst for my grand design. But he'll never truly understand. He'll never see the larger picture. He's too focused on the details. Too consumed by the superficial. He cannot grasp the true depth of my convictions. The true nature of my purpose.

He searches for a motive, a reason, an explanation for my actions. But there is no simple explanation. The issue is neither revenge, nor money, nor fame. It's about balance. It's about justice. It's about restoring the equilibrium of a world tilted on its axis by greed, vanity, and excess. It's about the silent screams of the forgotten, the overlooked, the neglected.

There's one last piece to the puzzle left. One ultimate trophy to claim. And when it's complete, when the narrative ends, the world will finally understand the true meaning of justice, the true price of vanity, and the chilling consequences of unbridled greed. The world will understand why it was necessary. They will finally understand the logic behind my actions, the precision of my methods. They'll understand that I was not just killing; I was cleansing. And they will see my true purpose. They will see the truth in my twisted vision. Because this is not about me. It's about them. It's about all of them. And you. You are watching, aren't you? You are complicit. You are part of this. You are next.

5

The rain hammered against the windowpanes, a relentless percussion accompanying the turmoil brewing within me. It wasn't remorse, not exactly. Remorse implied regret, a willingness to amend, a capacity for empathy I hadn't possessed since… well, since I could remember. What I felt was… a profound sense of satisfaction, tinged with a chilling emptiness. The emptiness that echoed the hollowness I'd found at the heart of my victims' lives. Their gilded cages, so meticulously constructed, were ultimately empty vessels, devoid of genuine meaning or connection. I filled that void, however briefly, with a stark and unsettling presence.

It started subtly, a whisper in the dark corners of my childhood. A disquiet, a simmering resentment towards the opulence I witnessed, the effortless ease with which those born into privilege navigated the world, oblivious to the struggles of those less fortunate. They moved through life like ghosts, untouched by the harsh realities that shaped the lives of others. Their wealth, their power, their beauty—it was all a façade, a carefully constructed illusion designed to mask a profound emptiness. I saw it then, even as a child, a sharp awareness that cut through the glittering veneer of their lives.

I remember the parties, the glittering balls, the endless stream of champagne and laughter. The air thick with the scent of expensive perfume and the murmur of hushed conversations, the clinking of crystal glasses, the shimmer of jewels against pale skin. But beneath the surface, I sensed a palpable coldness, a chilling disconnect. They were actors playing roles, inhabiting characters they themselves did not understand. They craved adoration, recognition, yet they remained profoundly alone.

My parents… they were players in this charade as well, their marriage a meticulously crafted performance, devoid of genuine emotion. Their love, a carefully staged illusion. Their concern was for appearances, for social standing, for maintaining their position in the rigid hierarchy of the elite. They loved their possessions more than each other, more than me. They always reserved their attention, like a precious gem, for those who could offer something in return. I was an afterthought, an inconvenient detail in their carefully curated lives.

Their neglect wasn't physical; it was emotional, a slow, insidious erosion of my sense of self, a gradual chipping away at my understanding of love, of belonging, of connection. The silence in their opulent mansion was deafening, the emptiness palpable. It was a void that I later learned to fill with a unique power, a dark and unsettling energy that emanated from the trophies I collected.

The thrill of the hunt wasn't merely about the acquisition of material possessions. It was about the power, the control, the meticulous orchestration of each death. It was a game, a carefully crafted narrative that unfolds with each carefully planned act. Detective Stone, with his dogged persistence, is but a pawn in this elaborate game. He's intelligent, almost understanding, but he lacks the crucial element: the ability to truly see the tapestry, the threads that connect each death, the narrative that underlies the apparent randomness.

The ritual was paramount, the precision crucial. The

trophies weren't mere souvenirs; they were symbolic representations of the essence I sought to extract from my victims, a distillation of their being, their power, their vanity. Each object held a significance far deeper than its material worth. Lady Beatrice's platinum blonde hair, Blackwood's diamond cufflink, Finch's ruby pendant—these were not just possessions; they were symbols of arrogance, ambition, and avarice, the very qualities I sought to challenge and ultimately dismantle.

But it wasn't simply a matter of dismantling. It was about understanding, about dissecting the pathology of the wealthy, the privileged, the untouchable. I studied them, observed them, learned their patterns, their vulnerabilities, their deepest insecurities. I immersed myself in their world, not merely to understand them, but to become them; to inhabit their skin; to experience the world from their perspective; to feel the hollowness at their core. Then, I extracted the essence, leaving behind only an empty shell.

The figurine, Anya Petrova's trophy, was different. It wasn't a symbol of material wealth or power, but a representation of the unattainable ideal; the relentless pursuit of perfection, the desperate attempt to fill the void within with something external. Their shallow existence and futile aspirations delivered a chilling testament. It's an intricate carving, a work of art, and yet its essence is chilling. It's a mirror reflecting the cold reality of the lives they lead.

Stone is getting closer. I can feel it. He's connecting the victims, the crime scene symbolism, and the unfolding narrative to solve the puzzle. The meticulous choreography of my actions is becoming apparent to him, yet he'll never understand my true purpose. He is a detective, not a psychologist. He seeks evidence; I offer a narrative. He sees the crimes; I expose the flaws.

The whispers continue, growing louder, more insistent. They're not just in the dark corners of my mind; they are all around me, in the silent hum of the city, in the rustling of the leaves, in the relentless patter of the rain. The forgotten, the neglected, and the invisible cry out silently; their voices echo in the opulent mansions of the wealthy, the halls of power, and the gilded cages of the privileged few. My actions are not about vengeance; they are about balance, a restoration of the equilibrium that has been so profoundly disturbed.

The last piece of the puzzle remains. The ultimate trophy awaits. And when the narrative is complete, the world will finally understand. They will see the truth, the chilling logic behind my actions, the unsettling beauty of my twisted vision. The profound emptiness at the heart of their world, the hollowness I sought to fill with a unique power, a different justice, will be understood by them. They will see the reason behind the silence, the whispers, the meticulously crafted choreography of death and destruction. They will understand the narrative, the twisted parable, the chilling symphony of blood and symbolism.

And you… you, who are reading this, you are a part of this. This involves you. You have witnessed the narrative; you have absorbed the essence of my actions, and in doing so, you have become a part of the story. Their guilt is equal to yours. Emptiness is something you share with them. You have understood, haven't you? The darkness has seduced you, haven't you? You crave this power too, this unsettling satisfaction. You feel the emptiness and the desire for a twisted form of justice, don't you? That same emptiness that motivated me. The same twisted desire to expose the hypocrisies of society. The same need to restore balance. And now you are next. You are the ultimate piece. You are the ultimate trophy. The collection is never truly complete, is it?

6

The chipped porcelain doll lay abandoned in the attic dust, its painted eyes staring blankly into the shadows. It wasn't a valuable object; a cheap, mass-produced thing, easily forgotten. Yet, it held a significance far beyond its intrinsic worth. It was a relic, a fragment of a memory, a shard of a shattered childhood. The cold porcelain sent a shiver down my spine as I picked it up, a visceral echo of the icy fear that had gripped me years ago.

The memory itself is fragmented, elusive, like a half-remembered dream. There are flashes of light, the jarring sound of shattering glass, the acrid tang of blood—not my own, but someone else's. A scream, muffled, distant, yet somehow piercing through the thick veil of my childhood amnesia. That night, the horrifying sounds shattered the mansion's opulent silence. It was a night of unimaginable chaos amid unparalleled luxury. A night that ripped through the veneer of perfection, the carefully constructed facade of my privileged world.

I was young, perhaps five or six, old enough to understand the concept of death, but too young to truly grasp its implications. The adults—my parents, or were they? The figures are hazy, their faces blurred, their voices lost to the mists of time—reacted with a chilling detachment. There was a frantic flurry of activity, hushed whispers, the frantic movement of shadows in the periphery. Then the silence descended again, heavier, more suffocating than before. They cleaned the scene and erased the evidence, but the memory, the visceral trauma, persisted. It gnawed at me, shaped me, warped my understanding of justice, of morality, of empathy.

The details remain elusive. Was it an accident? A deliberate act? Did my parents orchestrate the events of that night, or were they merely victims of circumstance? Perhaps they were both. Or perhaps it never even happened; perhaps it's just a manufactured memory, a carefully constructed narrative I created to justify my actions, a convenient explanation for the darkness that lives within me. The uncertainty fuels the narrative, allowing the ambiguity to breed suspicion and doubt.

The aftermath was as unsettling as the event itself. All that remained was the doll, a physical representation of lost innocence. The fragility of life and its ease of destruction served as a chilling reminder. The subsequent years were a blur of forced smiles, empty gestures, and the suffocating weight of unspoken truths. My parents, draped in their manufactured grief, moved through the motions of their lavish existence, oblivious to the chasm that had opened up within me. A chilling indifference replaced their affection. Their roles consumed them by the need to uphold their image, to project an air of flawless perfection. Their love was a performance devoid of warmth, genuine emotion, or genuine care.

I was alone. Truly alone, adrift in a sea of wealth and privilege, surrounded by people who were emotionally dead. The opulent mansion became a prison, each room a suffocating reminder of my isolation, the opulent decorations mocking the emptiness of my soul. The silence was deafening, far more terrifying than any scream. Their gilded cages, those perfect, crafted lives, did not differ from my prison.

It wasn't a lack of material possessions; it was a lack of connection, a profound absence of love and understanding. Their concern wasn't for my well-being; it was for appearances, for maintaining their position within society's rigid hierarchy. They were masters of manipulation, experts in the art of deception. They could charm the birds from the trees, yet they had no room in their hearts for their own daughter. Their cruelty was insidious; an emotional starvation that left me permanently scarred.

The memory of the doll became a symbolic representation of that shattered innocence. It was a physical manifestation of the void that had opened up within me, the emptiness that I would later seek to fill, not with love, not with connection, but with something far more sinister, far more destructive.

The opulent world around me became a breeding ground for my resentment. I observed, I learned, I absorbed the hypocrisy, the deceit, the shallowness that lay beneath the surface. The parties, the balls, the endless stream of champagne and meaningless laughter—they were all performances, carefully constructed facades designed to conceal a profound emptiness. I learned to mimic their behavior, to wear the masks they wore, to play the roles they expected of me. But beneath the surface, the darkness festered.

It was a slow burn, a gradual descent into darkness. The whispers started softly, a nagging discontent, a simmering resentment that grew stronger with each passing year. I saw the vulnerability of those who thought themselves invincible, the inherent fragility of their carefully constructed worlds. The emptiness at their core became the focus of my obsession, the target of my twisted ambition. The need for justice arose not from an evil intent but from a deep-seated desire for balance, a dark craving to redress the profound imbalance of their lives. Their privilege, I believed, was theft. A theft of opportunity, of resources, of basic human dignity from the less fortunate. My acts, therefore, were not merely murders; they were a form of twisted restitution.

The trophies I collect—they are not mere possessions. They are symbols, representations of the arrogance, the greed, the emptiness that I encountered. They are a tangible reminder of the lives I have taken, lives that were, in my twisted view, devoid of true value. The platinum hair, the diamond cufflinks, the precious stones—they are all pieces of a puzzle, fragments of a narrative that speaks to a greater truth, a truth that most people cannot, or will not, see.

The game continues. Stone, with his unwavering persistence, is still chasing shadows, failing to grasp the underlying narrative that dictates my actions. He chases facts, but I create an interesting story. He searches for evidence; I offer a masterpiece of psychological manipulation. He is a detective; I am an artist. And the last act is yet to unfold.

7

The porcelain doll, a relic from a fractured past, became a perverse talisman. Its cold, smooth surface mirrored the icy calm I cultivated, a mask concealing the simmering rage that had consumed me for years. The opulent world, once a gilded cage, now became my hunting ground. Each meticulously planned murder was not a random act of violence, but a calculated step in a long game, a twisted symphony of retribution.

I chose my targets carefully; each one represented a facet of the injustice I'd witnessed, a specific type of privilege that felt obscene and infuriating. There was Mr. Arthur Blackwood, the ruthless CEO who had driven his employees to ruin with his insatiable greed; his diamond cufflinks now rested in my collection, a testament to his shattered power. Then there was Lady Beatrice Worthington, her breathtaking beauty matched whose callous disregard for the suffering of others only; a strand of her platinum hair, almost impossibly fine, was woven into a macabre tapestry of my memories. Each victim was a symbol, a representation of a larger societal ill. I painstakingly orchestrated each death as a meticulous correction, restoring a balance I felt had been cruelly disrupted.

The murders themselves were performance art, meticulously staged to inflict maximum psychological damage, not just on the victims, but also on the city, the community, and indeed, on the very fabric of societal order. I orchestrated each scene like a play, carefully choosing the setting, the method, the message, the props. I left clues, breadcrumbs scattered across the city, a morbid puzzle for Detective Stone to unravel.

But my clues misled, designed to confuse, to challenge his intelligence, to taunt his relentless pursuit. They weren't simply clues; they were riddles crafted to amplify the feeling of helplessness that permeated his investigation. I manifested my control through them, reflecting his powerlessness. The more he investigated, the more he failed to understand my true motives, the more deeply he became ensnared in the psychological web I was weaving.

My fascination with psychology wasn't just a casual interest; it was a weapon, a tool I honed to perfection. I studied how my victims reacted: their fear, their despair, and the agonizing moments preceding their deaths. I savored the control, the power that surged through me as I observed the unraveling of their perfectly ordered worlds. It wasn't about the act itself, but the intricate choreography of the entire performance, the precise calculation of cause and effect. The thrill came from the game, the manipulation, the intricate dance of death.

Detective Stone, with his relentless pursuit, was an unavoidable part of the game. His presence, his frustration, his growing obsession—they all heightened the sense of drama to amplify the stakes. He was a necessary element, a catalyst, driving me towards my goal. I saw him not as an enemy, but as a fellow player, a necessary adversary whom my superior intellect and calculated precision ultimately outmatched, despite his immense skill and dedication. His desperation fueled my ambition, pushing me to even greater heights of psychological prowess.

His methods were predictable, based on logic and forensic evidence. He chased shadows while I manipulated light and shade, twisting the evidence to my advantage. He sought physical proof, while I constructed a narrative so interesting, so believable, that it overshadowed the facts. His pursuit only strengthened my determination, confirming the validity of my actions. I calculated my every move, designing them to draw him deeper into the game, making him a participant in my narrative, a silent witness to my reign of twisted justice. He became, unknowingly, another character in my grand design.

The emptiness of my childhood, the absence of genuine connection and affection, fueled my obsession. The opulent world, with its superficial charm and hollow relationships, was a constant reminder of that early trauma. My murders were, in a twisted way, a desperate attempt to fill that void, to restore a sense of balance to a world I felt had been unjust. It wasn't a lack of morality, but a perversion of it, a skewed sense of justice borne from deep-seated pain and a profound sense of betrayal.

The years of silence, the emotional starvation, the carefully constructed facade of a perfect family—these were the seeds of revenge. They nurtured a dark, consuming anger that bloomed into a calculated plan of retribution. It was a gradual process, a slow, insidious corruption that transformed a child’s pain into a woman's cold, calculated vengeance. The polished surfaces of the wealthy elite hid a moral decay, a vacuum of compassion that mirrored the emptiness at my core. This disparity fueled my twisted mission, turning the tables on the privileged, making them confront the consequences of their indifference.

My actions were not driven by hatred, but by a perverted sense of fairness. My desire was for a fairer world, one where the wealthy shared their advantages and powerful people felt the fear I'd always known. The ritualistic nature of the murders was not about sadism, but about the symbolic stripping of status, a methodical dismantling of the carefully constructed self-image of my victims. I meticulously curated each scene to amplify the psychological shock wave, not merely for the victim but for society drawing attention to the hypocrisy and injustices that remained hidden beneath the surface of polished society.

The game, however, was far from over. Detective Stone, with his unrelenting tenacity, remained a persistent thorn in my side. But his persistence only invigorated my resolve to sharpen my strategies. Every close call, every near miss, only fueled my ambition, refining my methods, solidifying my determination to see my twisted plan through to its devastating end.

The last act, I knew, would be the most spectacular, the most shocking, the most decisive. It would be a crescendo of violence and manipulation, a masterpiece of calculated chaos, orchestrated to leave an indelible mark on the city, on the world, and on Detective Stone himself. It was a game of cat and mouse, a deadly dance played out against the backdrop of a city oblivious to the horrors unfolding beneath the surface of its opulent veneer. And the last piece of the puzzle, the ultimate act of revenge, remained yet to be revealed.

8

The champagne flutes, delicate crystal etched with the Worthington crest, lay shattered amongst the silk sheets, a stark contrast to the pristine elegance of the bedroom. Lady Beatrice, a vision of ethereal beauty just moments before, was now a grotesque parody. Her platinum hair, once the envy of society, splayed across the crimson stain blooming on the Egyptian cotton. The strand I'd taken, impossibly fine and almost invisible against her skin, now lay nestled amongst my other trophies, a silent testament to my success. This was different. This was... refined.

With Alistair Finch, there had been a primal rage, a visceral need to obliterate the man who embodied unchecked greed. Beatrice, however, was a unique challenge, a more intricate puzzle. Her coldness, her indifference to the suffering of others, was a chilling mask concealing a deeper vulnerability.

I'd spent weeks studying her, observing her movements, analyzing her patterns, her weaknesses. I had infiltrated her world, becoming a ghost in her opulent machine, a silent observer, absorbing her every nuance.

I chose Lady Beatrice not for her wealth, though that was a considerable bonus, but for the sheer intellectual challenge she presented. Previous targets had been... predictable. I readily identified their vulnerabilities and easily mapped their routines. Beatrice was an enigma wrapped in silk and diamonds.

I conducted my initial observations from a distance. Weeks bled into each other as I followed her meticulously, charting her movements: the thrice-weekly visits to the botanical gardens, the Tuesday evening opera attendance, the random walks through less-frequented alleyways—each a piece of the puzzle.

I compiled a detailed dossier, not just of her habits, but of her subtle ticks—the way she adjusted her gloves, the slight tremor in her hand when agitated, the precise angle at which she held her fan. These weren't just mannerisms; they were keys. Infiltrating her world required a different strategy than brute force or simple bribery. I needed to become a part of her carefully curated ecosystem.

My opportunity arose through the Society for the Advancement of Botanical Studies—a group Beatrice was deeply involved with. I introduced myself as Dr. Thorne, a horticultural expert with important new research.

It was a fabricated identity, naturally, complete with forged credentials and a carefully constructed past. The deception was elaborate, requiring the fabrication of a past research career, the mastering of arcane botanical terminology, and the cultivation of a persona that was both knowledgeable and subtly charming.

The Society, thankfully, was rather exclusive, meaning vetting was rigorous, but my preparations proved thorough. My meticulously detailed research papers and my performance in front of the Society's board members, seasoned and discerning as they were, proved more than satisfactory.

Once accepted, it was a matter of patience. I studied her interactions with others, identifying her closest associates, their influence on her, and their potential vulnerabilities. My goal wasn't simply gaining proximity; it was about understanding the intricate web of relationships that she was woven into, to identify the most delicate threads I could sever to cause the most significant disruption.

I learned her preferences, her fears, her vulnerabilities, and most importantly, how to exploit them, all the while maintaining the façade of a harmless academic. The final stage, the execution itself, was…anticipatory. It was the culmination of months of meticulous planning and precision observation.

During the weeks spent studying her every move, I noticed the precise time the gardener left each evening, the subtle creak of her back gate, barely audible over the city's hum. That was my entry point. The security system, predictably, relied on outdated motion sensors easily bypassed with a strategically placed mirror reflecting the infrared beam.

Inside, the house was a labyrinth I'd mapped meticulously, identifying blind spots and the location of every security camera, their angles, and their recording schedules. It was almost artistic, the way everything fell into place.

The murder itself was a performance, a ballet of death. I chose a rare, highly toxic nightshade, its effects mimicking a peaceful sleep. I waited for her in her conservatory, surrounded by orchids and crystal champagne flutes, their perfume already intoxicating the air.

As she watered her prized bloom, I injected a carefully measured dose into the stem of a nearby lily. The flower's elegance formed a perversely perfect frame for the act. She admired the bloom a moment before it fell, a single petal gracefully touching her cheek as she succumbed, the poison working silently, swiftly, leaving no visible marks, no struggle.

I'd chosen the method carefully, a silent, swift execution, leaving no trace of struggle, no signs of a violent altercation. The death was serene, almost peaceful, a cruel irony that amplified the message: even in death, she remained an exquisite specimen, a perfect, lifeless doll. The porcelain doll I left on her chest, a grotesque mockery of her own lifeless perfection, was a final touch, a deliberate juxtaposition of innocence and brutality, a symbol of my triumph.

I had pre-planned my escape route, using the unlit, less-trafficked side streets. I changed into a different outfit I had stashed in my car, a nondescript jacket and hat concealing my appearance. I parked my car several streets away, providing a sufficient buffer.

I planned my route home carefully, avoiding the security cameras I knew were operational along the primary thoroughfares. Once home, I tossed the bloody clothes into a securely sealed bag and threw it in the trash, ensuring the next scheduled pickup would collect them. The entire process took less than thirty minutes. I felt a wave of accomplishment wash over me.

The following morning, the scene was… stunning. Lady Beatrice lay amidst her beloved orchids and shattered crystal, a scene of serene, almost melancholic beauty. The police, of course, would find no sign of forced entry. Her death would baffle the police; they might attribute it to a sudden heart failure. The beauty of the scene, the perfection of the plan, served as a counterpoint to the cold brutality of the act, a perverse juxtaposition that has haunted and thrilled me in equal measure. Elegance was of utmost importance. The success, exquisite.

Her death wasn't merely about ending her life; it was about exposing the hollowness beneath her flawless exterior, the emptiness behind the glittering facade. I had meticulously planned every detail, crafting a scene designed to highlight the contrast between her privileged existence and the brutal reality of her demise.

It wasn't just about killing her; it was about the performance, the meticulous orchestration of her downfall. This wasn't just for Detective Stone; it was about leaving a calling card for the entire city. This wasn't a random act of violence; it was a statement. A work of art crafted from the remnants of privilege and the raw, untamed chaos of revenge.

Detective Stone would undoubtedly focus on the similarities between the two murders. The meticulous staging, the careful selection of props, the absence of forced entry—all designed to lead him down a certain path, to reinforce his initial assumptions. But he would overlook the subtle differences, the nuances that revealed the evolution of my methods, the refinement of my techniques. He was a brilliant detective, but his adherence limited him to logic, to the tangible evidence. He failed to grasp the intangible, the psychological dimension of my game.

My understanding of psychology wasn't merely academic; it was an integral part of my methods. I expected his reactions, his lines of inquiry, and I adjusted my strategies accordingly. I expected his frustration, his obsession, and I used them to fuel my determination. He was a necessary element in my grand design, a constant presence pushing me towards my goal.

The trophies I collected were more than just mementos; they were symbols of power, tangible representations of my victories. Beatrice's strand of hair, almost invisible, woven into the macabre tapestry, represented the fragility of her dominance. It was a testament to my control, my ability to manipulate, to orchestrate events to my advantage.

Each trophy held a psychological significance, a reminder of my power, my intellectual superiority. They were tangible evidence of my triumph, not just over my victims, but over the systems, the institutions, the societal norms that allowed such imbalances of power to flourish.

This wasn't just about revenge; it was about sending a message, a warning. It was about dismantling the carefully constructed illusion of societal stability, exposing the hypocrisy, the cruelty hidden beneath the gilded surfaces of wealth and privilege. Each murder was a meticulously planned act of rebellion, a carefully orchestrated confrontation, a profound statement about justice and injustice.

The media frenzy surrounding the Worthington murder was predictable; predictable and satisfying. Headlines blared about a serial killer, a modern-day Robin Hood with a twisted morality, preying on the elite. The public's enthrallment, fascination, and terror were clear. The public was captivated by the macabre elegance of the crime scenes and the chilling mystery of the killer's identity. Their fascination fed my ego, their fear fueled my ambition. The fear was a tangible thing, a palpable energy that vibrated through the city.

Detective Stone immersed himself in the investigation, his obsession growing with each passing day. His frustration, his near misses, only strengthened my resolve. He was becoming increasingly erratic, his methods more desperate, his judgments clouded by the relentless pressure of the case. His growing obsession was a testament to my success. He was becoming consumed by the very game I had designed for him.

The psychological gamesmanship was exhilarating. I observed his every move, anticipated his every action. The clues I left were more than just indicators; they were deliberate distractions, misdirection crafted to steer his investigation away from the truth, deeper into the labyrinth of my design. Every subtle detail, every seemingly insignificant clue, was part of a larger strategy, carefully planned to mislead and manipulate.

He was getting closer. That much was undeniable. But closer only meant that my last act was drawing nearer. And the closer he came, the more intoxicating the game became. The thrill of evasion, the dance on the precipice of capture, was becoming almost addictive. The thrill of the chase, the exhilarating tension of near-misses, the knowledge that my control was absolute, was a potent narcotic.

I had already chosen my next victim. They were closer to Detective Stone than he could imagine, a connection I had carefully cultivated, a nexus point in the web of deception I had so meticulously spun. This wouldn't just be about revenge; it would be about a complete and utter dismantling of his world, a shattering of his carefully constructed reality. It would be the culmination of everything, a final, devastating performance designed to leave an indelible mark on the city, on his soul, and on the very fabric of reality itself.

The final curtain was about to fall. And Detective Stone, my unwitting co-star, would be the one to take the final bow. The applause would deafen, a symphony of terror and fascination echoing through the city and into the hearts of those who witnessed my masterpiece.

9

The city was a suffocating blanket of rain-slicked streets and nervous whispers. The media, fueled by the Worthington murder, churned out a relentless stream of speculation, each breathless report fanning the flames of public fear. Stone, however, remained stubbornly detached from the frenzy. His focus narrowed to a laser beam, cutting through the noise to the chilling heart of the investigation. He knew, instinctively, that this wasn't just a series of random killings; this was a meticulously crafted performance, a twisted game played out on the grand stage of the city itself.

He revisited the crime scenes, not just physically, but mentally. The opulent Worthington mansion, with its rain-soaked carpets and faint scent of lilies, echoed the chilling presence of Lady Beatrice as he walked. He imagined the killer, not as a nameless monster, but as an architect of death, a master puppeteer pulling the strings of the city's collective fear.

Stone felt a strange kinship with this unseen adversary, a perverse understanding that transcended the usual predator-prey dynamic. They were engaged in a complex dance, a deadly ballet of intellect and cunning. He was the hunter, yes, but he was also being hunted, his every move scrutinized, analyzed, anticipated.

The Finch case, the first victim, had been brutal, raw. This one, the Worthington murder, was… refined. The killer had grown, honed their technique, demonstrating a chilling mastery of psychological manipulation. The difference wasn't just in the method of death, but in the meticulously staged aftermath. It was as if the killer sought not just to extinguish life, but to create a masterpiece of macabre art, a chilling tableau designed to taunt and torment.

Stone found himself drawn to the psychological aspects of the case, far more than the forensic evidence. He spent hours poring over psychological profiles, studying the behavioral patterns of serial killers, searching for a clue, a hint, a flicker of understanding that could bridge the chasm between the tangible and the intangible. He was seeing the killer not just as a criminal, but as a formidable opponent, a supreme strategist who played upon his instincts, his prejudices, his very humanity.

The killer's calling cards, the carefully placed objects, weren't random. They were cryptic messages, puzzles designed to challenge him, to test his limits, to push him to the brink of obsession. The porcelain doll on Lady Beatrice's chest, the shattered crystal and serene lilies surrounding her, even the single, almost invisible strand of hair—each piece was carefully chosen, a piece in a larger, more sinister puzzle.

He noticed patterns, subtle repetitions, slight variations in the killer's methods. The meticulous staging, the choice of victims—wealthy, influential, untouchable—all pointed to a twisted sense of social justice, a perverse attempt to redress perceived imbalances of power. The killer wasn't just eliminating individuals; they were systematically dismantling a system, a social order that they deemed corrupt and unjust.

The more he investigated, the more he realized the killer was playing a game, a dangerous game of cat and mouse, with him as the unwitting pawn. He felt a growing sense of unease, a creeping suspicion that he was being manipulated, guided along a predetermined path. The killer wasn't just leaving clues; they were strategically misleading him, pushing him towards false assumptions, feeding his preconceptions.

His obsession grew with each passing day. He worked tirelessly, relentlessly, neglecting his sleep, his health, his relationships. His apartment became a chaotic mess of files, maps, crime scene photos, his personal life sacrificed at the altar of the investigation. Consumed by the hunt, he lost himself in the intricacies of the case, blurring the line between detective and hunter, pursuer and pursued. He wasn't just chasing a killer; he was chasing a phantom, a ghost, a reflection of his own relentless pursuit of justice. His belief grew that this hunt was, strangely, destroying him.

The killer’s methods had evolved. It was raw violence that defined some murders. The Worthington murder was a work of art. Subtle shifts and refined techniques hinted at an intelligent, calculating mind that could anticipate his every move. The precision and planning suggested a depth of understanding and an unsettling level of self-awareness.

He saw parallels between his own meticulous approach and the killer's carefully orchestrated crimes. He questioned his methods, his biases, the very foundations of his logic. The killer had not only outwitted him, but had mirrored his own approach, subtly mimicking his investigative methods. The uncanny similarity was a testament to the killer's understanding of him, an unsettling demonstration of their mental dominance.

Images from the crime scenes haunted his dreams, the faces of the victims, their empty eyes staring back at him from the darkness. He struggled to differentiate between reality and nightmare, his mind a battlefield of conflicting images and emotions. The line between his professional life and personal life had completely blurred.

The rain continued to fall, a constant drumbeat mirroring the rhythm of his own increasingly erratic thoughts. He felt a deep-seated sense of failure, a creeping fear that he was losing control, that he was being played, manipulated, and potentially outmatched in the very game he had set out to win.

His own obsession created a deadly psychological maze, and the killer was its architect. And he suspected that the last piece of this macabre puzzle was closer than he could ever imagine. He just didn't know how much closer. And that, he realized with a growing sense of dread, was the most terrifying thought of all. The killer was not just outside hunting him; but they were also inside him, influencing his thoughts, his emotions, guiding him closer to the inevitable end game.

The end game that was nearing a crescendo that even he could feel. And he knew that if he didn’t stop this, he was going to lose himself completely. And that frightened him more than any killer ever could.

10

The rain hammered against the windowpanes, a relentless percussion accompanying the unsettling rhythm of my thoughts. Detective Stone thinks he's so clever, so close. He sees patterns, symmetries, the careful choreography of my work. He almost understands. Almost. But he doesn't see the true power, the intoxicating essence I claim with each kill. He sees only the brutality, the meticulously staged scenes, the chilling trophies. He misses the heart of it all—the exquisite acquisition of beauty.

It's not just about the thrill of the hunt, the power surge of control. No, it goes much deeper than that. It's about the transference, the absorption. Each victim, each exquisitely chosen soul, possesses a unique beauty, a vibrancy that radiates from within. It's not just physical beauty, though, that plays its part. It's a deeper essence, a resonance of power, a potent cocktail of influence and charisma that I extract, ingest, and make my own.

Think of Beatrice Worthington, for instance. Her beauty was suffocating, a gilded cage of privilege and entitlement. She projected an aura of effortless superiority, a chilling indifference to the suffering of others. Her beauty was a weapon, a tool of manipulation. When I took her life, I didn't just claim her physical presence; I absorbed the essence of her power, her ability to command attention, to manipulate events, to remain untouchable. Serving as a conduit and vessel, the porcelain doll, a symbol of her flawless facade, allowed me to draw her essence into myself. The shattered champagne flutes? The delicate, crystalline fragments reflected the shattering of her illusion of invincibility. It was a ritual, a sacred act of consumption.

Before her, there was Finch. His beauty was unique, more subtle, more inherent in his intellectual prowess. A unique power. He held a certain allure, the intellectual kind that drew people in, that held sway over minds and institutions. He was a master manipulator of a different kind; his brilliance had built him an empire. His power emanated from his mind, his intellect. He was a fresh prey; he had always been several steps ahead in a board game of life. And I had to ensure he stayed that way. I had to ensure the game was not only fun and exciting but also one that he could never escape.

Each trophy is more than just a memento; it is a testament to my mastery, a tangible proof of my growing power. The strand of hair, the broken lipstick, the tarnished silver locket —they are conduits, vessels through which I absorb the essence of my victims, their unique beauty, their latent power. It's a gradual process, a subtle transformation. With each acquisition, I grow stronger, more confident, more assured of my ability to reshape the world in my image.

Stone may see the elegance in the staging, the calculated precision of my methods, but he cannot grasp the true significance, the transformative nature of these acts. He sees the patterns, the echoes, but not the resonance, the vibrations of power that ripple outward from each meticulously crafted scene. He sees the dead, but he doesn't see the life I'm creating, the new identity I'm forging from the essence of those I've taken.

He focuses on the forensic evidence, the tangible clues,

while I manipulate the intangible, the emotional landscape of the investigation itself. He's so focused on the hunt, so consumed by the chase, that he's blind to the game I'm playing, the subtle manipulations, the carefully orchestrated misdirections. I feed him clues, lead him down false trails, and he follows without question. It's almost amusing.

He chases shadows while I weave myself into the very fabric of the city, becoming a phantom, an enigma, a presence felt but never truly seen. His obsession fuels my power. The more he seeks me, the more I become. His relentless pursuit is a testament to my growing influence, a confirmation of my success.

And let's not forget the audience. You, the reader. You're implicated in this too, you know. The details entrance you, and the narrative captivates you. You crave the next act, the next reveal, just as Stone does. This macabre ballet invests you as much as it invests him. Your morbid curiosity, fascination with darkness, and need to understand all feed my power. You are not innocent bystanders; you are complicit, drawn into this dance of death, this grotesque waltz with destiny.

My actions are not random acts of violence. They are a deliberate, carefully calculated transformation, a systematic dismantling of the façade of societal perfection. I'm stripping away the illusion of invulnerability, exposing the shallowness and hypocrisy of the privileged elite. The wealthy, the powerful, the supposedly untouchable — I am their nemesis, their silent judge, jury, and executioner.

I am redistributing power, albeit in a grotesque and unconventional manner. I am a revolutionary, an agent of chaos, a harbinger of change. My methods are extreme, my motives complex, but I believe, deep down, that my actions are justified. I am correcting the imbalances, righting the wrongs, restoring a sense of balance to a world desperately in need of it.

The beauty I absorb is not just an aesthetic pleasure; it's a source of strength, a conduit to power. It is a symbol of control, dominance, and ultimate triumph. Each acquisition enhances my abilities, sharpening my intellect, strengthening my resolve. The more beauty I claim, the more I become it.

Stone thinks he is closing in, that he is about to apprehend me. He is close, perhaps, to the surface. He's piecing together the puzzle, identifying the patterns, recognizing the subtle repetitions in my methods. But he still doesn't see the totality, the grand design, the ultimate significance of my actions. He is a pawn in my twisted form of social justice. And soon, even he will know this truth, in his own way.

I don't intend to let him get close. Not really. The thrill of the chase is a part of the game, and the game is not ending soon. I might toy with him, lead him on, but he will never truly catch me. He's playing a game he can't win, and soon, he'll understand that it's not me he's hunting; it's himself. His own obsession, his own drive for justice, has set him on a path leading to his own destruction.

The rain continues to fall, washing the streets clean, cleansing the city of its guilt, leaving behind only the echoes of my actions, the lingering scent of power, and the enduring mystery of my identity. Soon enough, the last act will begin. And it will be one for the ages. One that will cement my legacy as an agent of profound change, the architect of my personal revolution, the master of beauty, power, and the perfect crime.

And you, dear reader, will be right there with me, watching it all unfold, consumed by its intoxicating allure.

After all, who can resist the exquisite power of beauty? Who can resist the intoxicating dance of death?

11

Here I am, confessing my crimes, laying bare my twisted motivations, and yet, I remain in control. You, the reader, are my captive audience, just as Stone, the detective, is my unwilling participant in this grand, macabre theater. I've woven a narrative so intricate, so interesting, that you find yourself not judging, not recoiling, but… intrigued. Perhaps even… admiring? The thrill of it all, the sheer audacity of my actions, the calculated precision of my methods—it's all part of the game, a carefully orchestrated symphony of fear and fascination.

And the humor? Oh, the delicious, dark humor of it all. The absurdity of it, really. A woman alone, reshaping the world, one exquisitely chosen victim at a time. The meticulously staged scenes, the carefully placed trophies—they are not just symbols of death; they are statements, bold proclamations of my dominance, my power. They are my calling cards, my signature on the canvas of societal hypocrisy.

Consider the case of Alistair Finch, the renowned art collector. He possessed a beauty so subtle, so understated, that it was almost invisible to the casual observer. His power wasn't brute force; it was the quiet, insidious power of wealth and influence, the power to shape narratives, to control perceptions, to dictate tastes. He was a collector of beauty, of exquisite objects, of rare and valuable things. And so, I collected him.

My game isn't just about the taking of lives; it's about the dismantling of illusions. I expose the hypocrisy of the wealthy, their self-serving narratives, their blind faith in their own invulnerability. Me, the antithesis disrupted their carefully constructed realities to their meticulously curated worlds. I am a force of nature, an unstoppable tide eroding the foundations of their gilded cages.

Stone, in his relentless pursuit, believes he's unraveling a complex puzzle. He sees the connections, the patterns, the echoes in my methods. Some perverse attraction draws in him, no, but by a deep-seated need for justice, for resolution. He is a man consumed by his work, consumed by me. His obsession fuels my power, his frustration provides me with endless amusement. He is so focused on the hunt, so blinded by his own righteous fury, that he cannot see the bigger picture. He chases shadows while I remain firmly entrenched in the heart of the game.

But the game isn't just between Stone and me. It's a game that involves you, the reader. I've invited you into my world, shared my thoughts, my motivations, my twisted justifications. I've given you a glimpse into the darkness, the profound dissatisfaction that fuels my actions. And by sharing this with you, by involving you in the narrative, I've made you complicit. Your morbid fascination, your insatiable curiosity, your need to understand — it all fuels me. It feeds my power.

The rain, a constant companion throughout this narrative, washes away the evidence, cleansing the streets, leaving only the lingering echoes of my actions. But it doesn't wash away the memories, the impressions, the indelible mark I've left on the city, on its inhabitants, and on you. The haunting echoes of my words and the chilling implications of my actions linger with you, the reader. You must grapple with your own complicity and fascination with the darkness.

My methods are extreme, yes, but they are also precise, deliberate, and artistic. Each kill is a performance, a carefully choreographed act designed to expose the hypocrisy and shallowness of those I target. I select my victims with care, choosing those whose power and influence have caused the most harm, those who embody the societal imbalances I seek to correct.

There's a twisted satisfaction in watching Stone chase shadows, in knowing that he's so close yet so far from the truth. He's trapped in a maze of my making, a labyrinth of clues and red herrings, all leading him farther and farther away from the answer he seeks. His frustration, his obsession. It's all fuel for my game. The hunt consumes him, lost in the chase, and he cannot see the intricate dance he is performing.

He thinks he's smart, thinks he can outwit me, but he's wrong. He's playing a game he can't win. My grand design has the perfect foil: my pawn, him. And every step he takes, every clue he discovers, only brings him closer to his own downfall. The truth will eventually reveal itself, but not in the way he expects. Not in how it will bring him any closure or satisfaction. His understanding of the game is only limited to its surface, unaware that he is the actual victim of my grand design, a willing participant in my psychological warfare.

I am a puppeteer, and Stone is my most prized marionette. He dances to my tune, oblivious to the strings that bind him. He is so close, yet so far away, so obsessed with the chase that he doesn't see the trap closing around him. His pursuit is not a hunt; it is a self-destructive obsession, a journey to his own ruin. I have created a game that not only satisfies my hunger for justice but also serves as an instrument of exquisite psychological torture.

There are still pieces to be moved, pawns to be sacrificed. And you, the reader, will be right there with me, witnessing the unfolding drama, drawn into the heart of the darkness, experiencing the thrill of the chase, the delicious suspense, and the intoxicating allure of the unknown. In the end, grapple with the ultimate question: are you a spectator or a participant in this deadly game? And what are the consequences of your choice? What truly is your role in the grand tapestry of my twisted, beautiful, and utterly deadly design?

12

The rain lashed against the windowpanes of my apartment, mirroring the tempest brewing inside me. Stone's relentless pursuit was grating on my nerves, a persistent buzz that threatened to disrupt the carefully orchestrated symphony of my actions. He was closing in. I could feel it, the tightening grip of his investigation like a constricting boa constrictor. But he was still playing my game, dancing to my tune, oblivious to the strings I so expertly manipulated.

Stone, in his methodical, almost obsessive approach, saw patterns where others only saw chaos. He saw the connections, the echoes, the meticulous craftsmanship of my killings. Understanding my work's artistic nature, he saw its deliberate choreography of death and the carefully constructed tableaux I left behind. He was closing in on the underlying philosophy, the twisted morality that justified my actions.

The fear, the thrill of it all, fueled me. This dance of death, this terrifying game of cat and mouse, was exhilarating, a high unlike any other. The closer he came, the more the stakes rose, intensifying the game's inherent tension. It was a high-wire act, a ballet of death, and the risk, the potential for failure, only added to its appeal. He believed he was closing in; he believed he was winning. The irony, of course, was delectable.

My response to his progress was simple, elegant, and utterly devastating. I added another layer to the game, an extra dimension of complexity that would throw him off his scent, deepening his frustration and fueling his obsession. I left a calling card, a message, a subtle provocation at the scene of my next killing.

It was a simple object, a child's toy soldier, meticulously positioned amidst the scattered debris of my latest victim—a prominent politician whose arrogance and self-serving ambition had finally become unbearable. The soldier, a symbol of manufactured heroism and misplaced authority, stared defiantly at the rain-slicked pavement. A silent challenge to Stone, an invitation to continue playing.

The implications were subtle, layered, and deeply unsettling. The child's toy, in its innocence and simplicity, represented the corruption and betrayal inherent in the political arena. It was a commentary, a twisted social commentary that was both humorous and deeply disturbing. They strategically placed the carefully chosen toy; it served not only as a provocation but also as a clue—a meticulously planned piece of disinformation, a breadcrumb leading him down a winding and ultimately misleading path.

I watched Stone's frantic movements through my surveillance network—a vast and intricate web of carefully placed cameras and listening devices that allowed me to monitor his every move. His team worked tirelessly, poring over evidence, dissecting clues, desperately seeking connections. Their desperate search for answers, constantly frustrated by the ever-elusive truth, caught them in a vortex of their own making.

Stone himself, consumed by the investigation, became increasingly erratic, his dedication bordering on fanaticism. His obsession grew, the lines between his professional and personal life blurring into a dangerous haze. Sleep deprivation and relentless pressure had taken their toll, rendering him susceptible to manipulation.

He was losing himself in the chase, becoming increasingly detached from reality, his judgment clouded by his relentless desire to apprehend me. This obsessive pursuit was precisely what I had intended. He was becoming my unwitting accomplice in my grand design, a participant in the macabre game that was slowly consuming him.

His frustrations became my fuel, his desperation, my source of amusement. I watched him spin his wheels, getting closer and yet further away from the truth. It was a slow, deliberate torture, a psychological game of attrition that played on his deepest insecurities and vulnerabilities. He was close enough to feel the thrill of the chase, yet far enough to never truly grasp the complexity of my intricate scheme. My intricate scheme trapped him, a prisoner in his obsessive quest for justice.

I selected each piece of evidence carefully; each clue was a deliberate misdirection, part of my psychological warfare against him. I provided him with enough to keep him chasing shadows, leading him down the wrong path, making sure that he was always one step behind. It was a masterful orchestration, a delicate balance between providing hints and throwing him off the trail. I was a puppeteer, and he was my marionette, dancing to the rhythm of my manipulations.

I trust a few individuals within the department. There's Sergeant Booth, a man I've known since our days at University. His current position in the records division provides him access to a wealth of information.

Then there's Officer Munch, a young patrol officer who owes me a significant debt from a past personal matter. He's always been eager to prove himself and will often pass along observations from his shifts.

Finally, Detective Rollins, a veteran working narcotics, occasionally shares information in exchange for favors. He's always appreciated my discretion and ability to remain unbiased. These contacts provide me with a consistent flow of information, though their reliability and motivations naturally vary.

My methods were extreme, my actions brutal, but they were also precise, artistic, and thoroughly effective. Each murder was a performance, a statement, a bold proclamation designed to expose the hypocrisy and the shallowness of the elite. I was not merely a killer. As an artist of chaos, I sculpted destruction. I was a force of nature, reclaiming what was stolen from those deserving better.

The game was far from over, the dance of death far from its climax. There were still pieces to be moved, more pawns to be sacrificed. The last act was yet to be played, and Stone, my devoted accomplice in this gruesome play, was unknowingly leading the way. He was closer than he realized, and yet still hopelessly lost, completely unaware of the grand design unfolding around him. His obsession was my strength, his blindness my weapon.

The scene was being carefully arranged, a culmination of my calculated steps, a spectacle designed to deliver the ultimate shock, an unforgettable finale. And the audience? You, the reader, watching with bated breath, utterly unaware of what awaits you. Are you ready?

13

I chose Senator Harrison's residence in Georgetown for its predictable security. I observed his routine for weeks, noting his jogging schedule, the arrival times of his staff, and the patterns of his visitors. His security detail was minimal, rotating between two officers, each with predictable shift changes.

I selected a Thursday, knowing his schedule was less hectic on that day. I acquired a replica key, a simple matter given the lack of sophisticated security systems. The house was older, relying on traditional locks. I timed my entry for 11:17 PM, just before his usual bedtime and well before the security detail changed.

I moved silently, careful not to trigger any alarms. Senator Harrison’s study was on the second floor, easily accessible from the unlocked back door that had never been a subject of security consideration. I found him asleep in his aged leather wing-backed chair, a lit cigar between his fingers, and a half-read book resting on his chest. The letter opener sat on his desk—a sharp, weighty instrument.

My actions were swift and deliberate. I raised the letter opener, plunging it into his chest. The first thrust met resistance, but I pressed again, deeper. Blood spilled quickly and generously, staining his Persian rug and the tailored suit he'd worn to the Senate that day. The mess of blood splattering nearby surfaces didn't faze me; I was prepared. I used cleaner to wipe away traces of my fingerprints, concentrating especially on the letter opener's handle.

After disposing of the murder weapon in a pre-selected location, I exited the residence the same way I entered. I left no trace of my presence, other than that which I could not entirely remove. My planning had been meticulous; my execution is efficient.

The air hung thick and cloying in Senator Harrison's opulent study, the scent of old leather and expensive cigars battling with the metallic tang of blood. Harrison lay sprawled across his Persian rug, a crimson stain blooming across his tailored suit, a grotesque parody of his carefully cultivated image. His eyes, wide and unseeing, stared up at the ornate ceiling, their former arrogance replaced with a stark, chilling emptiness.

I had chosen the setting deliberately, a space that reflected Harrison's arrogance and self-importance. The sheer opulence, the symbols of power and privilege surrounding him, served only to highlight the fragility of his life, the utter insignificance of his power in the face of death.

My trophy this time was different, a departure from the previous acquisitions. Instead of a single object, a tangible symbol of vanity, I took something far more intangible, something far more personal. I took his dark brown hair dye, used to hide his perfectly coiffed natural silver hair, representing years of a carefully crafted youthful public image of ambition ruthlessly pursued. The power, the perceived strength, vanished with its removal. The emptiness left behind was satisfying.

The method itself was unsettling, even for me. I'd used a

tool I haven't in the past—a sleek, obsidian letter opener, its blade honed to razor sharpness. The precision with which I wielded it was a testament to my control, a demonstration of my power. The act of killing wasn't about rage, not completely. It was about artistry, control, a carefully calibrated dance of death.

Amid this carefully staged scene, amidst the scattered papers and overturned furniture, I placed my calling card. This time, it was not a single object, but a collection of items, each carefully chosen to amplify the symbolic impact. A child's toy soldier, a symbol of contrived heroism and misplaced authority, and a small, tarnished silver medal, representing the hollow achievements that made up his life's work. The message clearly showed that insignificance can reduce even the most secure and powerful lives, exposing their false pretenses.

Stone, I knew, would dissect these objects, searching for meaning, for connections. Stone would discern the pattern, the escalating intensity of my 'messages,' but he would remain lost, hopelessly stuck in the mire of my carefully constructed misdirection. This time, my misdirection went even deeper. I designed the choice of objects not only to confuse him, but to subtly direct him toward a completely false conclusion—a carefully laid trap to waste his time and lead him further from the truth.

My fascination with the psychology of manipulation, honed over years of intense study and a lifetime spent observing human behavior, was the driving force behind my elaborate games. I wasn't simply killing; I was crafting narratives, sculpting stories in blood and handpicked objects. Stone, with his intense focus, was playing right into my hands. His obsession, his tunnel vision, was my greatest weapon.

Leaving the scene, I felt a familiar surge of exhilaration, the adrenaline coursing through my veins like a potent drug. The risk, the inherent danger, fueled me, sharpened my senses. But there was another element, a deeper satisfaction derived from observing Stone's increasingly frantic attempts to understand my method. The psychological impact of my actions would linger, etching itself into the fabric of the city, into Stone's psyche, and into the consciousness of those who witnessed, either directly or indirectly, the unfolding of my twisted drama.

The next day, I watched from afar as Stone and his team swarmed Senator Harrison's opulent study, their movements frantic, their faces etched with a mixture of grim determination and dawning bewilderment. The carefully positioned cameras in my surveillance network provided me with a clear view of their actions. They were like ants scurrying around a complex mechanism they didn't understand, their efforts futile, their investigations ultimately leading them further from the truth.

Stone's obsession was escalating, his sleeplessness and the strain visible in his gaunt face. His demeanor was becoming increasingly erratic, his judgment clouded by the relentless pressure and the weight of the investigation. He was cracking, the strain of his relentless pursuit taking its toll. This was precisely what I wanted; I needed him to lose his objectivity, to surrender to his obsession. He was my perfect audience.

The initial police reports focused on the items I'd left behind, the random collection of objects. News outlets were abuzz with speculation, focusing on the symbolism, the potential political motives, the random nature of my next victim. The experts on crime shows on TV were stumped, offering various contradictory theories, all missing the crucial element, the deeper psychological pattern underpinning my actions.

I fed them more scraps of information, more breadcrumbs leading them down winding paths that led nowhere. I leaked false leads, planted disinformation, guiding their investigations towards red herrings. I controlled the narrative, directing their focus away from the truth, keeping them perpetually one step behind. It was a masterclass in psychological manipulation, a game played on the highest stakes.

Meanwhile, Stone's professional life had bled into his personal life, his sleep disrupted, his relationships strained. His obsession had become all-consuming, transforming into something akin to a destructive addiction. He was becoming as much a prisoner of the game as I was. His attempts to capture me were not just a professional pursuit; they had become a personal vendetta, a desperate struggle against the unraveling of his own sanity.

His pursuit of me wasn't simply a pursuit of justice; it was an obsessive need to solve the puzzle, to understand the workings of my twisted mind. He wanted to unravel the intricate web of my psychological manipulations, to grasp the depths of my perverse logic. In a way, he was understanding me, though his understanding was flawed, distorted by his own obsession. I trapped him, completely engrossed in the intricate game, unaware of the much larger, more terrifying picture I had designed.

And that, my dear reader, was the beauty of it all. The intricacy, the carefully crafted layers of deception, the deliberate misdirection—it was all part of the grand design, the elaborate theater of my actions. Stone, unknowingly, was a vital part of this performance. He was the audience, the protagonist, and the unwitting accomplice in my terrifying game of cat and mouse. And you, the reader, were also a participant, silently observing, unknowingly entangled in the web of my creation. The last act awaits.

14

You think you're watching, don't you? A detached observer, safely nestled behind the pages of this… confession? A voyeur peering into the twisted mind of a monster. But I'm telling you, dear reader, you're wrong. Dead wrong. You are more than just an observer; You've chosen to read this, to delve into the darkness, to unravel the threads of my meticulously crafted narrative. That makes you complicit.

Think about it. Every page turned, every sentence absorbed, is a tacit agreement, a silent nod of approval. You crave the thrill, the frisson of fear, the unsettling fascination with the forbidden. Exploring the darkest corners of the human psyche and glimpses into the abyss are things you relish. You are, in your own way, addicted to the violence, to the power, to the meticulously choreographed dance of death I present. You're not just reading a story; you are taking part in a perverse ritual.

And what of Stone? In my grand game, he, the relentless detective and embodiment of order and justice, is merely the most visible pawn. He's driven by his obsession, blinded by his need to understand, to unravel the intricate tapestry of my mind. This brilliant and perceptive detective is now caught in my web, entangled in the strands of my carefully constructed narrative. He chases shadows, chasing me, chasing the ever-elusive truth. But the truth, my dear reader, is far more disturbing than anything he could ever imagine.

His frustration mounts with each meticulously planned act. He grasps at clues, meticulously examining each piece of the puzzle, convinced he's close to the solution. He is, of course, utterly wrong. The closer he gets, the more he delves into my intricate game of psychological manipulation, the further he drifts from the reality I have carefully crafted for him, the reality I have carefully crafted for you.

You see the patterns, don't you? The escalating intensity, the subtle symbolism embedded in each crime scene. The choice of victims, the carefully selected trophies. You're piecing it together, constructing your own theories, trying to understand the logic—or lack thereof—that drives me. But that's precisely what I want. I need you to engage, to take part, to become inextricably bound to this narrative.

My trophies are not mere objects; they are extensions of my victims, vessels containing their essence, their power, their very being. I absorb them, assimilate them, becoming stronger, more powerful with each act. I feed on their fear, their desperation, their last moments of terror. This is not mere sadism, this is sustenance. This is my twisted form of evolution, of transcendence.

And what of you? What do you absorb from these pages? What part of my twisted reality clings to you, stains your mind, lingers long after you've finished reading? Do you feel a perverse sense of satisfaction, a grim sense of completion with each carefully constructed chapter? Do you feel the thrill of the chase, the intellectual stimulation of trying to unravel the complex mechanisms of my mind, the chilling thrill of inhabiting my thoughts? The complicity is insidious, a slow-burning poison that you willingly consume with every word.

I understand your fascination. The darkness of the forbidden, the things society deems abhorrent, draws you in.

You are, in a sense, a reflection of me. We share a perverse fascination with the grotesque, the macabre, the unsettling beauty of death. You find a strange fascination in my ability to orchestrate these elaborate performances, in my ability to manipulate not only Stone but also the very fabric of society itself.

But your fascination is a dangerous game, my dear reader. It's a game that blurs the lines between observer and participant, between witness and accomplice. It's a game that could consume you, leaving you as twisted and broken as my victims. Are you willing to risk it?

The climax approaches. Soon, the consequences will be inescapable, the stakes impossibly high. And you will confront the chilling reality of your own involvement. You'll see it reflected in your own eyes, in the quiet horror that chills you to the bone, the quiet recognition of the darkness you've embraced, the darkness you've actively sought.

Stone, in his relentless pursuit of justice, is unwittingly chasing a reflection of himself. He delves deeper into the abyss; the darkness pulling him in, threatening to consume him entirely. His investigation isn't just a pursuit of justice, it's a desperate attempt to understand, to make sense of the chaos, to grasp the perverse logic of my actions.

But he'll never truly understand. Because the genuine horror lies not in my actions, but in the reflection they cast upon him, upon the society he represents, and most significantly, upon you, the reader. My game isn't just about killing; it's about exposing the inherent darkness that lies within all of us, the darkness that allows us to be passive observers, to indulge in our fascination with the morbid, to turn the pages, and continue reading, despite knowing that we're taking part in something terrible, something deeply wrong.

You've read this far, haven't you? This meticulously crafted vortex of deception and violence has drawn you into its world of darkness. You have indulged in the morbid curiosity, the perverse thrill of it all. The adrenaline coursing through your veins mirrored my own exhilaration and twisted sense of triumph. You're as guilty as I am, my dear reader. You're as much a part of this game as Stone, as my victims, as myself.

In the end, you will face the chilling truth—the horrifying realization that your fascination and complicity make up active participation. It is active participation. You are, in a sense, a murderer, just like me.

15

The city lights blurred into a smear of crimson and gold through the rain-streaked windowpane. Below, the city throbbed, a pulsating heart oblivious to the quiet symphony of death I had orchestrated. Each victim, a carefully chosen note, resonated in the discordant composition of my life's work. They were not merely individuals; they were symbols, reflections of a society that glorifies excess while ignoring the suffering of the many. As the executioner, I was their grim reaper to the gilded cages, symbols of privilege.

I am, after all, merely a mirror reflecting their own ugliness back at them. A grotesque, distorted reflection, perhaps, but a reflection. They built their towers of ivory, their empires of indifference, and I built my edifice of revenge upon the foundations of their hypocrisy. Each murder was an act of reclamation, a dismantling of the structures they so meticulously constructed. A twisted, brutal form of social engineering.

Look at them, those who believe themselves to be untouchable. Their lives, meticulously curated for public consumption, are a farce, a grotesque pantomime of happiness and success. Beneath the veneer of perfection, the rot festers. The emptiness, the moral bankruptcy, is palpable. I merely exposed their rotten core, laid bare their hypocrisy for all to see. My methods may be extreme, brutal even, but they are effective. They are a necessary shock, a jolt to their complacent existence.

Consider the trophies. They are not mere souvenirs, not grisly mementos of my crimes. They are fragments of their souls, tangible representations of the power and essence I've absorbed. Each one is a piece of a shattered puzzle, a puzzle that reveals the grotesque truth about them, about us.

Think of the lock of platinum hair. Snatched from the icy grip of the socialite, now forever preserved in resin, encasing the hair like an eternal memory in a locket. Its delicate chain now draped around my neck, a subtle reminder of her shallow existence. Or the diamond cufflinks, emblems of a corporate titan's ruthlessness, now adorning my wrist. These are not mere trinkets; they are tools, vessels through which I channel their power, their very being. I feel their energy, their arrogance, their cold indifference seeping into my veins, fueling my actions.

The locations, the timing, the selection of victims—all a testament to my mastery of the game, a game played on the very edge of sanity. The police, with their archaic methods, their limited understanding, are nothing more than puppets, dancing to a tune I have composed. They chase shadows while I weave a web of deception around them, ensnaring them in the intricate tapestry of my mind.

But even I am subject to the intoxicating thrill of the chase. The thrill of the hunt, the careful planning, the precise execution. The adrenaline, that electrifying rush that accompanies each successful performance, is addictive. It fuels my creativity, sharpens my focus, allows me to orchestrate my acts with chilling precision. And yet, despite my meticulous planning, there is a certain seductive element of unpredictability, a wild, untamed energy that propels me forward. The intoxicating fear of my victims, the desperation in their eyes, their silent pleas for mercy—all of this only heightens the pleasure, intensifies the experience. It is a perverse addiction, a dark craving that fuels my actions.

The media frenzy, the public outcry—it's all predictable, all part of the play. The endless speculation, the outlandish theories, is a source of dark amusement. They flail, desperate to understand, to find a pattern, a motive, anything to make sense of the chaos. But the truth is far more subtle, woven into the fabric of their own lives, their own values, their own hypocrisies. Their fear, desperation, and utter inability to comprehend the depths of my intent reflect the truth.

Stone's unwavering dedication is admirable, but his obsession borders on self-destruction. He's caught in a game he cannot hope to win, a game where the rules are constantly shifting, the stakes endlessly rising. He's blinded by his need for closure, consumed by the puzzle he can't solve. His meticulous investigation, his earnest efforts, only highlight the flaws in his thinking, in his approach, in his worldview. He's chasing a phantom, a reflection, a carefully constructed illusion.

He seeks order in a world I've deliberately thrown into chaos. He seeks justice in a system that has long since ceased to function. His pursuit of me is a pursuit of himself, a desperate attempt to confront the darkness that simmers beneath the surface of his own perfectly ordered world.

And you, dear reader, what part do you play in all of this? As silent observer, a voyeuristic audience, and a participant in a macabre performance, you are present. You are the one who turns the page, the one who continues reading, the one who indulges in the dark fascination, the morbid curiosity. You are as much a part of this story as I am.

Your complicity is insidious, as slow-burning and deadly

as any poison. In your own way, you reflect the darkness that lives within us all, the darkness that lets us passively consume and watch the horrors unfold without thought of the consequences. This is not just a story, dear reader; it is an act of confession, of revelation, a mirror reflecting not just me, but you.

There is one last victim, one last reflection, one last piece of the puzzle to be revealed. And when the dust settles, when the last note fades, the horrifying truth of your own complicity and the chilling reflection of the darkness you have willingly embraced will confront you. The reflection staring back at you will be more horrifying than anything I could have ever done.

You have delved into this darkness to explore the abyss. You have allowed yourself to be drawn into my world, to become entangled in my intricate web of deception. In the end, you will bear witness to the chilling conclusion, a reflection of the darkness that lies within you, a darkness that you have so willingly embraced.

16

The flickering neon sign of the all-night diner cast a sickly yellow glow on Detective Stone's face, highlighting the deep grooves etched around his eyes. He hadn't slept properly in weeks, the killer's meticulous game playing out in his mind like a broken record, each gruesome detail replaying itself in vivid, horrifying clarity. He pushed the lukewarm coffee around in its chipped mug, the bitter taste mirroring the bitterness that had settled deep within him.

The city, usually a chaotic symphony of noise and movement, now felt like a vast, empty stage, devoid of life and meaning. The vibrant energy that had once fueled him, the drive that had propelled him through countless investigations, was fading, replaced by a gnawing emptiness, a void that seemed to grow larger with each passing hour.

The killer's taunts, subtly woven into the crime scenes, echoed in his mind—not spoken aloud, but whispered in the wind, a constant, insidious presence. He was losing himself in the complex corridors of the case, losing his grip on reality.

The police department, once his sanctuary, now felt like a suffocating cage. His colleagues, once his trusted comrades, now seemed distant, their concerns for his well-being sounding hollow, their words lost in the cacophony of his own spiraling thoughts. They saw the exhaustion, the haunted look in his eyes, but they couldn't see the insidious tendrils of madness that were slowly consuming him, binding him to the killer's twisted game.

He tried to rationalize, to maintain some semblance of objectivity, to adhere to the principles of criminal investigation he had so meticulously learned. He meticulously examined each crime scene again and again, searching for a clue, a detail, anything that could unlock the mystery. But the more he delved, the more confused he became. The killer's actions defied logic, transcended any known pattern, existing in a space beyond the realm of rational understanding.

His superiors, initially impressed by his relentless pursuit, were growing concerned. His methods had become unorthodox, borderline reckless. He was working alone, isolating himself, losing himself in the depths of the investigation. Stone survived on coffee and willpower, getting little sleep. He was blurring the lines between investigator and obsessive, detective and lunatic.

The killer's psychological manipulation was a masterclass in deception, a complex game of cat and mouse, played not just with the police, but with the entire city. Stone constantly questioned his own perceptions, his own judgment. Was he losing his mind, or was the killer deliberately driving him to the brink of madness? Was he simply a pawn in a grander, more sinister game than he could ever comprehend?

He saw the killer's influence seeping into his dreams, vivid nightmares filled with blood, ritual, and the chilling gaze of the killer. Waking in a cold sweat, his heart pounded, the images burned into his mind. He unconsciously mimicked the killer's rituals, his actions becoming increasingly erratic, his behavior alarmingly erratic. He'd stare at reflections, examining his own image, searching for signs of the encroaching darkness.

His apartment had become a shrine to the investigation, a chaotic jumble of files, crime scene photos, and scribbled notes. Pictures of the victims plastered the walls, each face a ghostly reminder of the escalating horror. He slept on the floor amidst the mounting chaos, his mind racing, his body exhausted, his spirit broken. Doubt, confusion, and fear shattered his once-orderly world, replacing it with a labyrinth.

The line between reality and delusion had blurred, leaving him in a state of perpetual disorientation. He questioned the reliability of his own senses, the accuracy of his own perceptions. Stone wondered if he was losing his mind, or if the killer was manipulating his very essence. He questioned everything, even his own sanity. Was he still pursuing justice, or had he become a puppet in the killer's deadly game?

Stone started seeing patterns, connections, where none existed. He'd find meaning in coincidences, interpreting chance encounters as part of a larger, more sinister plot. He'd spend hours poring over seemingly insignificant details, searching for hidden meanings, losing himself in a vortex of speculation and conjecture. His obsession was no longer about catching the killer; it was about understanding the killer, about unraveling the intricate mechanics of their mind.

The city lights, once a source of inspiration, now felt like accusing eyes, judging his descent into madness. The constant rain, a relentless torrent of water, seemed to mirror the endless deluge of thoughts washing over him, drowning him in a sea of uncertainty. Stone's relentless pursuit of the truth, a pursuit threatening to consume him entirely, trapped him, not the killer's cunning. He realized the killer wasn't just manipulating him; the killer was mirroring his own obsessions, his own flaws, amplifying them, magnifying them until they were all-consuming.

He, the relentless detective, the champion of justice, was becoming the very thing he was hunting, a testament to the insidious power of obsession, a cautionary tale of a mind broken by the relentless pursuit of truth. Stone was no longer the hunter. He was the hunted, a victim of his own ambition, consumed by his own darkness. He realized the chase wasn't about solving the case; it was about finding himself, or what remained of him, in the aftermath of the relentless, consuming hunt.

Stone's obsession had become a mirror, reflecting his own deepest fears, his own darkest vulnerabilities. He was drowning in a sea of his own making, a testament to the destructive power of unchecked ambition and the fragility of the human psyche.

The city had become a desolate wasteland, a reflection of his own internal chaos. And in the quiet hours of the night, alone in his apartment surrounded by the remnants of his investigation, he finally understood: the true crime wasn't the murders; it was his own descent into madness. The game was over, but the devastating consequences had just begun. The darkness he sought to expose consumed him, leaving Stone lost and broken.

17

The rain lashed against the windows of the secluded cabin, mirroring the tempest brewing inside me. The air hung thick with the scent of pine and something else… something metallic and sharp, clinging to the back of my throat like the taste of blood. This time, it was different. This time, the ritual felt… final.

He was an artist, renowned for his breathtaking landscapes and paintings that captured the raw beauty of the untamed wilderness. He saw beauty where others saw only chaos, a stark contrast to the ugliness I sought to expose. He was my antithesis, a beacon of light in a world I found hopelessly marred by darkness. His name, Theo Graves, was now just a whisper, a memory to be savored and then discarded.

The preparation was meticulous, a symphony of calculated movements. I'd studied his routine, his habits, his vulnerabilities. He was a creature of habit, predictable in his solitude, his sanctuary a fortress only to his own sensibilities. His isolation was his undoing. I observed him for weeks, a ghost in his periphery, learning his rhythm, his preferences. Blending into his shadows, I watched him, absorbing his aura, his essence. I expected his every move.

I chose the secluded cabin because of its isolation, a

crucial factor in my plan. Weeks turned into months of observation. I learned his routine: the exact time he left for his morning jog, the grocery store he frequented, the pattern of his evening walks. I studied the layout of the cabin, its windows, the security system, if any. I discovered a gap in surveillance, hidden by overgrown bushes, perfect for my approach.

The key was gaining a duplicate. Lock-picking was a skill I lacked; I employed a distraction, a small, carefully placed fire near his property line. The ensuing controlled chaos provided cover for me to lift a key impression using readily available modeling clay, which was then used to generate a functional duplicate using readily available supplies.

The night of the killing, the weather cooperated; a heavy, persistent thunder storm masked the sound. I arrived under the cover of darkness, slipping silently through the obscured blind spot. The duplicate key worked flawlessly, silent even to my sensitive ears.

Inside, Theo Grave was at his easel, back to the door. He was painting, lost in his creative process, unaware of my presence, oblivious to the fate that awaited him. His canvas, a vibrant portrayal of a serene forest, was a cruel irony. I was a storm about to destroy his peaceful paradise.

I moved with practiced ease, careful to remain outside the reach of any motion detectors I had ruled out were present. I moved like a shadow, blending into the darkness, my footsteps muffled by the thick carpet of fallen leaves. His easel, bathed in the faint glow of a single lamp, illuminated his profile, the intense concentration etching lines of exhaustion onto his face. He was a masterpiece himself, a monument to fragile beauty. I savored the moment, the exquisite tension before the climax. The anticipation was a drug.

The sculpting knife was his own; the small, delicate blade, perfect for my purposes, mirroring his artistic nature. Its sharpness was a counterpoint to the gentle brushstrokes he employed on his canvases. It was a twisted parody of creation, a perverse act of artistic expression. He never saw me before the knife found its mark, the precision stroke delivered to the canal of his right ear.

His movements were instantaneous, a desperate lunge, but his strength was no match for the speed and force of my action. The struggle was brief; a sharp, piercing cry and then a last gasp of breath, a desperate attempt at self-defense, ending as quickly as it began. I was in and out. The rain washed away any evidence of my presence, leaving only a tragic tableau.

Afterwards, I disposed of the knife separately. I incinerated the clay impression. The rain washed the earth clean. I left nothing to trace me. My planning was precise. The lack of any emotional response, even during the execution, was a chilling confirmation of how far I'd come. The satisfaction felt was not something positive but rather the confirmation of a well-executed plan, nothing more.

There was no real scream, no prolonged agony. It was swift and clean, a sudden cessation of a life that had become a symbol of the injustice I sought to rectify. His eyes, filled with a mixture of confusion and terror, widened as he met my gaze, recognizing the cold steel of the blade before the inevitable. The finality of it was profoundly satisfying, a clean break from the life he had lived.

Afterward, the ritual began, a sinister performance staged within the intimate confines of his isolated abode. This time, the trophy was a single paintbrush, carefully selected from his collection, its bristles still bearing traces of vibrant color. I carefully cleaned it, ensuring no trace of blood or other evidence remained. It was a symbol of his talent, his skill, his artistic expression—all stolen and transformed into something sinister. The brush would now become a part of me.

I left the cabin as silently as I had entered, leaving behind the storm and the carnage. The rain washed away any trace of my presence, obscuring the evidence as effectively as the darkness had shielded my actions. The storm raged on, washing away the blood and the truth, a silent accomplice to my act.

The following days were a blur of meticulously planned activities, designed to ensure my safety and to conceal the reality of my actions. I destroyed any evidence that could link me to the crime, meticulously cleaning any remaining trace, discarding incriminating objects in strategically chosen locations.

I changed out of my blood-stained clothes behind an abandoned theater deep in the city, tossing them into a dumpster overflowing with refuse after soaking them in bleach, washing away any potential DNA. My shoes, I left near the construction site a few blocks over—somewhere I knew the workers would clear out debris soon.

The feeling of power was intoxicating. I felt reborn, cleansed, revitalized. Each victim, each act of violence, was a step closer to restoring balance in this imbalanced world. Each trophy was a physical manifestation of this power, the essence of their lives distilled and absorbed.

The investigation intensified. Detective Stone was relentless, his obsession growing with each passing day. His pursuit mirrored my own—a relentless drive, fueled by a morbid fascination with the macabre. His determination was a testament to his skill, his tenacity, his complete and utter dedication to the cause.

Yet, my work was impeccable. I left no trace, no clue, no fingerprint. I existed only as an idea, a shadowy figure lurking in the margins of society. From the shadows, I manipulated events, the unseen hand, the force.

The media frenzy that followed the fourth murder escalated to a fever pitch. Fear, the whispers of the mysterious killer fueling public hysteria gripped the city. Each news report was a testament to my success; each speculative article served as a reminder of my power. I manipulated the narrative from afar, planting subtle clues, leading the investigation down blind alleys. I orchestrated events, ensuring their focus remained away from the truth, away from the person they really wanted to find.

Days blurred into nights. Sleep was a luxury I could not afford; even in rest, my mind was busy working, analyzing, planning. My actions were deliberate, carefully calculated, each move designed to further confuse and mislead the investigation. The investigation was a game, and I was masterfully controlling the board.

The fourth victim, the artist, served a different purpose than the others. He was not merely a symbol of the wealth and privilege I so despised. He was a representation of something larger, something deeper. His reflection showed me the beauty and artistry found in destruction. His life, his art, became the fuel for my next phase.

I saw my work differently now. I was not merely a killer; I was an artist of destruction, an architect of chaos. The investigation's events were easily twisted to my will; I was a master of psychological manipulation. Detective Stone's obsession blinded him from the larger truth.

The trophies, I realized, were not mere souvenirs; they were the building blocks of a larger work of art, a masterpiece of death and destruction. Each object, carefully chosen and preserved, was a piece of the puzzle, a symbol of the power I held over the lives and minds of those around me.

The confession was just a performance, a theatrical display of control and manipulation. It was a way to further taunt and engage Detective Stone, to draw him deeper into the game. I watched him, fascinated by his descent into madness, his growing obsession. He was a mirror, reflecting my darkness back at me. His obsession was proof of my success.

The game, however, was far from over. The last victim would be a testament to my skill, my power, my artistic control over life and death.

18

The meticulous cleaning of the cabin felt almost ritualistic in itself. Each wiped surface, each discarded item, was a testament to my control, a silent affirmation of my power. The storm had subsided, leaving behind a damp chill and an unsettling stillness that clung to the air like a shroud.

I stood there, bathed in the pale light of the early morning, feeling the lingering adrenaline ebb away, replaced by a chilling calm. The artist's lifeless form lay where I'd left it, a tableau of unsettling beauty.

Detective Stone, I knew, wouldn't be far behind. His unhealthy obsession was as much a part of my game as the killings themselves. He was a necessary component, a vital piece in the intricate puzzle I was constructing. His frustration, his desperation, fueled my sense of power.

The media, of course, was already in a frenzy. The 'Ghost of the Pines', they called me. A phantom, a specter haunting the wealthy elite of the city. Each sensationalized article, each breathless news report, felt like a validation of my twisted vision. I manipulated the narrative from the shadows, feeding them carefully selected tidbits of misinformation, guiding their investigation down pre-planned paths. The more they searched, the further they moved from the truth.

I had carefully constructed a false trail, a web of deceit so intricately woven that even I sometimes struggled to unravel it. It was a masterpiece of misdirection, a symphony of lies designed to disorient and mislead. I'd left behind fragmented clues, carefully placed anomalies that pointed towards innocent parties, deflecting suspicion and attention away from myself.

But the real deception was far more subtle, far more insidious. It was a manipulation of perception, a distortion of reality, playing upon the inherent biases and assumptions of those who investigated me. I planted suggestions, subtle inferences, designed to shape their interpretations of the evidence, to solidify their preconceived notions. I used their own prejudices against them.

For instance, there was the matter of the missing security footage. The security cameras around the artist's cabin had mysteriously malfunctioned on the night of the murder. A simple act of sabotage, expertly carried out weeks in advance, providing a perfect alibi.

The media, quick to latch onto simple explanations, dismissed the malfunction as a coincidence, a technical glitch in an old system. Stone, however, was more perceptive. However, I cleverly redirected even his suspicions, my carefully laid clues guiding him toward alternative, ultimately fruitless, explanations.

I played upon the public's fascination with the paranormal. Whisperings of ancient curses, supernatural occurrences, permeated the news cycle, adding a layer of mystical obfuscation to the case. The whispers amplified my mystique, transforming me from a mere killer into a legend, an enigma.

I started small. A few anonymously posted online forum

comments mentioning strange noises near the old mill. Then I subtly leaked grainy, indistinct photographs to local news outlets, claiming they depicted shadowy figures. I created a fake social media account to post fabricated eyewitness testimonials, each one slightly more elaborate and sensational than the last.

My next step was to plant ‘evidence’—strategically placed objects near the cabin, like oddly arranged stones or flickering lights easily misinterpreted. I used burner phones to call in fake emergency reports, describing unexplained phenomena. The local newspaper, hungry for a story, ran with it.

The cumulative effect of these carefully orchestrated events gradually built a narrative of intense paranormal activity around the cabin, attracting attention from paranormal investigators and tourists alike. It all unfolded precisely as I planned, a steady progression of fabricated events designed to create a believable, albeit completely false, story of haunting.

As the investigation intensified, I intensified my manipulation. The pressure mounted on Detective Stone. He made mistakes, to overlook crucial details, to become consumed by his own obsession. His descent into obsession was a masterpiece of its own, a testament to my psychological prowess. His every action became predictable, his frustrations becoming tools in my game.

The shifting narratives were not just a means of evasion; they were a form of psychological warfare. I was not just evading capture; I was conducting a symphony of chaos, directing the actions of the detectives, and even influencing the public's perception through the cleverly crafted leaks and the manipulative whispers. The very act of deception became a source of intoxicating power.

But the act of deception required not only manipulation, but a deep understanding of psychology and human nature. I delved into each potential suspect's psyche, creating narratives that catered to their specific vulnerabilities, their hidden insecurities. I fed them information that confirmed their own biases, creating a feedback loop of suspicion that ultimately led them nowhere. The detective's wife was a prime example.

Stone’s wife, Sarah, a renowned therapist, possessed an uncanny ability to perceive subtle cues, to read between the lines. I leveraged this, planting seeds of doubt in her mind, whispers of infidelity, hints of dark secrets.

I found an old, slightly crumpled receipt tucked inside a book at the library—a pricey restaurant, the kind Detective Miller would never take his wife to. I subtly photographed it and anonymously sent it to her, along with a similarly anonymous, innocuous-looking postcard showing a nearby hotel.

Then, a week later, I sent a slightly blurry photo appearing to show a woman's hand holding what looked like a diamond ring near a luxury car parked outside the same hotel. I never contacted the Detective's wife directly, leaving her to draw her own conclusions.

Her suspicions, naturally, turned towards her husband, further consuming his time and diverting the investigation away from me. The subtle hints of infidelity, however, were not entirely false. They were carefully constructed half-truths, carefully designed to fuel her existing anxieties.

The constant back-and-forth, the shifting perspectives, blurred the lines of reality. Were the police reports accurate, or were they part of the larger deception? Was Detective Stone's growing obsession a product of his own paranoia or a result of my manipulation? And what about my narrative? How much of it was truth, and how much was a carefully constructed fiction designed to enthrall, to captivate, to mislead?

The line between truth and fiction blurred. My narration itself became a weapon, a subtle form of psychological warfare. I shifted perspectives seamlessly, creating a fragmented narrative that reflected the fractured reality I had constructed. I used the reader's own biases against them, implying complicity, subtly suggesting that their fascination with my actions was a tacit endorsement.

The power derived from this manipulation was intoxicating. I was not merely a killer; I was an artist, sculpting the very fabric of reality, bending minds to my will. The investigation was becoming a collaborative piece of art, a masterpiece of psychological deception, with Detective Stone unwittingly playing the role of the tormented protagonist.

The real masterpiece, however, was yet to be unveiled. The last victim, the ultimate sacrifice, awaited. This act would be the culmination of my work, a testament to my complete and utter control over life and death.

The last piece would not only shock Detective Stone but also you, the reader, who was complicit in the journey. The ultimate deception was not just in the murders, but in the implication of you yourself, a subtle acknowledgment of the dark fascination that fueled your own journey through this narrative.

19

The crisp autumn air bit at my exposed skin as I watched the city lights twinkle below. From my vantage point, high atop the unfinished skyscraper, the city sprawled beneath me like a meticulously crafted diorama. Each shimmering light represented a life, a story, a potential victim. But tonight, tonight was different. Tonight, the game reached its climax.

Detective Stone, ever the persistent hound, was close. His relentless pursuit had become almost comical in its predictability. He chased shadows, chasing phantoms I deliberately crafted, while the real game unfolded far beyond his grasp. He was a pawn, a necessary component of my carefully orchestrated finale.

You, dear reader, are another.

I've noticed your fascination, your morbid curiosity. Your silent complicity in this narrative. You've followed my actions, absorbed my justifications, perhaps even felt a flicker of understanding, a twisted empathy. You've become intimately involved in my game, whether you admit it. And now, the last act is upon us.

I didn't choose my last victim at random. Oh no, this was a carefully selected piece, a crucial element in the ultimate deception. Someone who, in the grand tapestry of my masterpiece, would weave together every thread, every lie, every carefully placed clue. Someone you know and trust.

The irony, of course, is exquisite. You, the reader, the voyeuristic observer of my perverse actions, are about to become a participant, a silent witness to the last act. Even if you don't realize it, you're implicated. You have, through your fascination with my twisted narrative, become inextricably entwined with my destiny.

The last act involves a seemingly simple exchange. An anonymous package, delivered to your doorstep. Inside, a small, elegantly wrapped box. Don't open it yet. Let the anticipation build, let the suspense twist the knife deeper into your curiosity.

The package contains a single, perfect crimson rose. Its petals, delicate and flawless, conceal a tiny, almost imperceptible tracking device. It's a seemingly insignificant detail, easily overlooked, a microscopic thread in the intricate tapestry of my deception. But it's crucial. It allows me to know your location, to monitor your every move. To observe your reaction to the unfolding events.

You see, I've tailored this last act to play upon your inherent biases, your own vulnerabilities. I've carefully crafted this narrative to manipulate your expectations, to lead you down a predetermined path. Your perception, your understanding of reality, is all part of the trap.

The rose is more than just a tracking device. It's a symbol, a representation of the beauty I have sought to possess, the power I have sought to absorb from my victims. It reflects the inherent beauty and power you, the reader, hold in your fascination with my actions. It is a memento mori, a reminder of your own mortality, your own complicity in my twisted journey.

The rose is also a form of psychological warfare. It's a subtle suggestion, a seed of fear planted in the fertile ground of your imagination. It's a silent whisper in the dark, a constant reminder that you're being watched, that your every action is being monitored. This subtle psychological warfare plays into the deepest fears of humanity; the fear of the unknown, and the fear of being controlled.

And that, my dear reader, is the point.

The next piece of the puzzle involves Detective Stone. His obsession, his relentless pursuit, will ultimately lead him to a dead end—a meticulously crafted red herring. I've guided his investigation down a blind alley, a carefully constructed maze of misinformation, designed to keep him off balance, to amplify his frustration and desperation. It's a slow, deliberate game, designed to test his patience, to push him to the brink of madness.

His frustration is my fuel. His obsession is my power. He will be close, yet frustratingly far from the truth. His desperation will only heighten the drama, to increase the tension, to intensify the climax. He will chase a ghost, while the real action unfolds elsewhere, completely unseen by his watchful eye.

The package, the rose, the tracking device - these are all elements of a far larger narrative, a psychological chess game where you are a crucial pawn, entirely unaware of your position on the board. This subtle manipulation, this calculated play upon your emotions and expectations, is the ultimate test of my prowess as an artist of death. It is the zenith of my manipulation.

The last act will not involve violence. At least, not in the conventional sense. It's a far more subtle, far more insidious form of violence. A psychological assault designed to shatter your preconceived notions, to challenge your very understanding of reality. It's about control, about power, about the intoxicating thrill of manipulating minds, of bending wills, of twisting perceptions.

Remember the artist? The careful selection of my victims has always been deliberate, a finely tuned collection representing specific aspects of society's decadence. The artist was a masterpiece in his own right, a representation of the superficiality and the artificiality of the upper echelons of society. His death was symbolic; an act of rebellion against the superficial.

This last act is unique. It’s more personal. It is about the unraveling of reality itself. The blurring of lines between truth and fiction, between perpetrator and observer. It's a game of mirrors, reflections and shadows, designed to leave you questioning everything you thought you knew. Your complicity is essential. Your fascination is my weapon.

The ultimate trap is not physical. It’s mental. It’s a masterpiece of deception, woven from the very fabric of your own expectations. The question you must ask yourself isn't who I am, but who you are. What type of person seeks out this narrative? What does it say about you, the reader, that you've followed my story this far?

The game has just begun.

20

The investigation continues, but the detective remains oblivious to the true nature of the crime. He chases the ghost of a physical perpetrator, while the genuine horror lies in the reflection staring back from the page.

Detective Stone reviewed the case files for months, noting the inconsistencies in the initial investigation. The lack of forensic evidence at the crime scenes, coupled with the victims' undisturbed belongings, pointed towards a killer with a meticulous approach and intimate knowledge of the victim. This suggested the killer was someone close to each victim, or someone who had carefully observed their routine.

Stone's investigation ultimately led him to the killer, a neighbor who had consistently provided seemingly insignificant details during the initial questioning. Her alibi, however, contained minor discrepancies that Stone found suspicious. He obtained a warrant to search her residence.

Upon arriving at her house, Stone observed nothing outwardly unusual. The house was tidy, showing no signs of a recent struggle. The flickering gaslight cast long shadows across Detective Stone's weary face, highlighting the dark circles beneath his eyes. He hadn't slept properly in weeks, the relentless pursuit of this elusive killer gnawing at his sanity.

He'd expected a dramatic confrontation, a violent struggle, but the reality was far more unsettling, a chilling dance of intellect and depravity. He found her not in some dimly lit alleyway or abandoned warehouse, but in a surprisingly ordinary suburban home, nestled amongst manicured lawns and picture-perfect houses. Recognizing the irony, he paused.

She sat in a high-backed chair, a single crimson rose in a crystal vase, the only splash of color in the starkly minimalist room. She looked… ordinary. Not the monstrous figure he'd conjured in his mind during countless sleepless nights. No wild eyes, no crazed laughter. Just a woman, perhaps a little too composed, a little too serene for the gravity of the situation.

The crimson rose, a stark contrast to the sterile white of the room, pulsed in Stone's peripheral vision. He rubbed his temples, the throbbing a dull counterpoint to the unsettling silence. The woman, the killer, sat serenely, a sphinx-like enigma. He'd spent months chasing shadows, piecing together fragments of a meticulously crafted narrative, yet the core remained elusive. He felt like an archaeologist meticulously excavating a tomb, only to find the sarcophagus empty, its secrets buried deeper than he could ever imagine.

Stone focused on the victims, their lives, their connections, trying to find a common thread, a unifying factor beyond their wealth and status. He'd studied their social circles, their habits, their vulnerabilities. He'd examined the trophies he had found—a single, perfect ruby from one, a lock of platinum hair from another, an intricately carved figurine from a third—searching for clues, for a pattern, for a connection beyond the obvious, to tie these to the victims.

But it was the pattern itself that was the key. The victims

weren’t the key. The random selection of victims, the disparate backgrounds, the seemingly unconnected lives—these were not random at all. They were a carefully curated collection, designed to create a specific psychological effect, a meticulously planned mosaic of tragedy.

Stone realized the trophies weren't merely souvenirs, they were components of a larger, far more sinister puzzle. He saw the connections not between the victims, but between the trophies themselves. They were not symbols of the victims, but fragments of a larger narrative, a chilling metaphor for the decay he'd observed in society.

The woman, the killer, had not merely murdered; she'd composed a symphony of death, a macabre opera performed for an audience she never directly confronted. Each victim was a note, each trophy a carefully chosen instrument. She played on their vulnerabilities, their vanity, their greed, their hubris.

The realization struck him with the force of a physical blow. The victims weren't just wealthy; they were all connected to him, tangentially, through various charitable events, social gatherings, and acquaintances. He had met them, chatted with them, and seen them as members of the elite he often criticized privately, never imagining his own involvement.

The killer had played a twisted game, not just of murder, but of mirrors. She reflected society’s flaws back upon itself, using its most privileged members as instruments to expose its own hypocrisy and decadence. She had chosen her victims not because of any personal vendetta, but because they represented the very flaws, she sought to highlight. They were not simply symbols of a decaying system, but symbols of the system's complicity in its own demise.

Stone revisited his initial investigative work, painstakingly sifting through the evidence, the reports, the crime scene photographs. He saw the subtle connections, the links between the seemingly disparate elements. The killer had left her fingerprints, not in the literal sense, but in the very fabric of the society she sought to critique. She had interwoven her narrative into the social tapestry of the city's elite.

The last piece of the puzzle fell into place with a sickening thud. The killer wasn't some anonymous figure lurking in the shadows. She was someone he knew, someone he had encountered many times, someone he'd dismissed as being merely another cog in the machine of high society. It was a woman named Serena Holloway. A philanthropist, renowned for her charity work, admired for her elegance and grace, and seemingly the very epitome of the virtuous life the killer claimed to restore.

The irony was suffocating. Serena Holloway, the champion of the disadvantaged, the protector of the vulnerable, was the very embodiment of the twisted justice she so vehemently claimed to administer. Her meticulously crafted public persona masked a chilling secret, a dark heart that beat in time with the rhythm of her gruesome murders.

The realization was not a sudden epiphany, but a slow, creeping horror, an icy dread that wrapped around him like a shroud. It was not just the shocking revelation of her identity, but the chilling implication of her actions. She had not only murdered; she had manipulated, controlled, and ultimately, exposed the hypocrisy of a society that readily embraced her public persona, while remaining blissfully unaware of the sinister truth lurking beneath the surface.

He looked at the killer, Serena, her eyes devoid of remorse, but flickering with a disturbingly smug satisfaction.

He saw the subtle arrogance, the superiority of a skilled artisan who had completed a masterpiece, a symphony of death composed and conducted with chilling precision. The trophies were not merely objects but parts of a larger artistic statement, a grim commentary on the societal decay she sought to expose.

Stone felt the weight of his failure, the crushing realization that his own biases and preconceived notions about justice and morality had blinded him. He had been chasing a phantom, a carefully constructed illusion, while the actual monster walked amongst them, cloaked in virtue and philanthropy.

But the horror ran deeper than the simple revelation of Serena's identity. The woman had not only manipulated him, but she had also manipulated the narrative itself, using her confession as a weapon, pulling the reader into her twisted game. She had woven a web of deception so intricate, so masterful, that the distinction between reality and fiction had become hopelessly blurred. The reader, like Stone, had become a pawn in her game, a willing participant in her macabre drama.

This wasn't a confrontation, but a revelation, a chilling exposure of complicity. It was a mirror reflecting the darkness within ourselves, the morbid fascination we harbor for the forbidden, the unsettling allure of the criminal mind. Serena Holloway had not simply committed murder; she had exposed the darkness within us all, a darkness we choose to ignore, a darkness that enables the very injustices she claimed to correct.

The game was over, but the lingering unease, the haunting realization of our own participation in her twisted narrative, would remain, a constant reminder of the fragility of truth, the seductive power of manipulation, and the chilling implications of our own morbid fascination.

The final act was the unsettling awareness of our shared culpability, the silent acknowledgment of our complicity in the narrative of a woman who redefined the concept of the perfect crime: one that transcends the physical realm and delves into the deepest recesses of the human psyche, twisting our own perceptions and leaving us questioning everything we thought we knew.

The silence in the room was heavier now, filled not with the emptiness of solved mystery, but with the weight of unspoken truth. The aftershocks of the revelation would resonate long after the dawn broke, painting the city in a new and disturbing light.

21

The steel glinted briefly in the afternoon sun as Detective Stone secured the handcuffs around Serena Holloway's wrists. Her hands, clasped in front of her, were unremarkable for the slight tremor noticeable only upon close observation. Without resistance, they led her to the back of the unmarked police cruiser. Stone checked the restraints before entering the driver's seat. The car's siren remained silent as it pulled away from the curb, its tires meeting the asphalt with a muted thud.

The journey to the precinct was uneventful; a straight route punctuated only by the rhythmic thump of the tires and the occasional blink of a traffic signal. Serena sat rigidly, her gaze fixed on the passing scenery. Upon arrival, the cruiser pulled smoothly into a designated parking space, and Stone unlocked the rear door, escorting Ms. Holloway directly into the station.

The sterile white of the interrogation room seemed to amplify the silence, a silence thick with unspoken accusations and the lingering scent of fear. Serena, her composure as flawless as ever, met Stone's gaze with an unnerving calmness. The game appeared over, or so it seemed. The physical game, at least. Her chillingly masterful performance continued to resonate, its echoes reverberating in Stone's mind.

He'd expected a confession, a breakdown, a flicker of remorse. Instead, he found an almost serene acceptance, a chilling satisfaction in her eyes that sent shivers down his spine. It was the look of an artist contemplating their finished masterpiece, an unsettling creation born of twisted logic and a chillingly precise understanding of human nature. Justice, she'd claimed, had been served. But whose justice? And at what cost?

"You believe you've brought justice," Stone finally said, his voice raspy, the words catching in his throat.

He felt the weight of the unspoken questions, the burden of the unsettling truth that had unfolded before him. The trophies, the meticulously chosen victims, the carefully orchestrated narrative—it was all part of a larger, more sinister design. A design that had entangled him, the reader, and perhaps even society itself, in its intricate web.

Evelyn smiled, a slow, deliberate curve of her lips that revealed nothing of her inner turmoil.

"Justice," she echoed, her voice a low, melodious purr, "is a subjective concept, isn't it, Detective? A fluid entity, shaped by perception, defined by perspective. You sought justice for your victims, for society. I sought a different justice, a more… fundamental one."

She leaned forward, her eyes intense, her gaze piercing. "I eliminated the parasites, the leeches who thrived on the suffering of others. They were the ones who corrupted the system, who perpetuated the inequalities that blight our society. I merely sped up their inevitable demise, exposed the hypocrisy that allowed them to flourish."

Her words hung in the air, a poisonous concoction of justification and manipulation. Stone grappled with the unsettling truth of her statement. The victims had been, in their own way, symbols of societal decadence, figures who had benefited from a system they had helped to corrupt. Were they truly innocent? Or were they complicit in the very injustices they unknowingly embodied?

The line between justice and revenge blurred, becoming as indistinct as the boundary between reality and the carefully constructed narrative Evelyn had woven around her crimes. She had not simply murdered she had performed a twisted act of social commentary, a grotesque theatrical production where the victims were both actors and audience.

Stone thought of the ruby, snatched from Allistair Finch, who had risen to wealth through dubious means. He recalled the platinum hair, symbolizing passion and deceit, taken from Lady Beatrice, known for her callous disregard for the poor. Each trophy, each victim, was a carefully selected component of a larger design, a perverse mosaic of social critique.

Serena's justification, as twisted and morally reprehensible as it was, forced Stone to confront the uncomfortable truths embedded within her narrative. The system she'd sought to dismantle was undeniably flawed, riddled with inequalities and hypocrisy. Her victims, while victims, were not saints. They were complex individuals, products of a system that rewarded avarice and punished compassion.

"You're a monster," Stone finally whispered, the words choked with a mix of disgust and a disturbing sense of recognition.

It wasn't merely the murders that repulsed him, but the chilling intelligence, the meticulous planning, the psychological manipulation that had allowed her to escape detection for so long. She hadn't just killed she'd orchestrated a masterpiece of deception, a symphony of death played on the very strings of society itself.

Serena chuckled, a sound both chilling and strangely captivating.

“Perhaps,” she conceded, a hint of something akin to amusement in her voice. “But even monsters can serve a purpose. I exposed the rot, the festering corruption at the heart of this city. I forced you, Detective, and everyone else, to confront the uncomfortable truths we’d rather ignore.”

The words hung in the air, heavy with implication. She was right, of course. Her actions had forced a reckoning, a confrontation with the hypocrisy and inequalities that underpinned the city's opulent facade. She’d shattered the illusion, exposing the darkness beneath the gilded surface, but at a horrific cost. She achieved her ‘justice,’ a sinister parody of the ideal, through violence, manipulation, and death.

The question of justice remained unanswered, a haunting specter that loomed over the aftermath of her capture. Stone knew that her prosecution, judgment, and condemnation were certain. The legal system would grind its gears, dispensing its own brand of justice. But would that be true justice? Would it erase the unsettling questions her actions had raised? Would it reverse the physical and psychological damage?

The room felt smaller now, the silence more oppressive. Stone looked at Serena, her composure unwavering, her gaze steady. He saw not a monster, but a warped reflection of society itself, a mirror held up to expose its darkest flaws. Justice, he realized, was a far more complex and ambiguous concept than he’d ever imagined.

It was not a simple equation of punishment and retribution, but a tangled web of moral dilemmas, ethical complexities, and unsettling truths. And in the twisted logic of Serena Holloway's game, the true cost of justice remained chillingly unclear, a lingering shadow that haunted the very notion of what it means to truly serve justice.

The last act wasn't a courtroom drama; it was a quiet reckoning, a confrontation not only with Serena, but with the darkest aspects of society and the reader's own complicity in its perpetuation. The story left the question of justice unanswered; it was amplified, echoing in the unsettling silence of the interrogation room. A dissonant chord in a symphony of moral ambiguity.

Had justice been served? The answer, like the killer herself, remained elusive, a chilling enigma wrapped in the guise of social commentary and a shockingly effective manipulation of perception. Even in the sterile confines of justice, the ambiguity remained, a lingering doubt like the phantom scent of blood in a room meticulously cleaned.

Serena's legacy, her twisted brand of justice, would forever haunt the edges of the investigation, a stark reminder of the complexities of morality and the terrifying power of a mind determined to redefine the rules of the game.

The silence held more than answers; it held questions, unanswered, haunting, chilling, and as potent as the blood spilled in the name of her skewed definition of justice.

22

The harsh whiteness of the room closed in around me, suffocating and uninviting, a stark contrast to the swirling chaos within me. Stone's departure left a vacuum, a silence filled with unspoken accusations, yet oddly, a sense of relief. The game, as I called it, was over. Or was it? The arrest, the confession—all carefully orchestrated moves in a far larger game. One played not just with Stone, but with you. With all of you.

You, the reader, have been privy to my thoughts, my justifications, my twisted, darkly beautiful vision of justice. You've followed my narrative, absorbed my words, and perhaps even felt a flicker of understanding, a perverse admiration for the elegant precision of my actions. Don't deny it. I see it in the way you turn the pages, in the way you linger over the details, the trophies, the victims. Your implication is as deep as Stone's and that of the system I aimed to destroy.

Consider the ruby, shimmering in its evidence bag, a symbol of wealth, stolen from a man whose cruelty knew no bounds. Did the taking of that ruby—its exquisite, flawless surface cool against my skin—not bring you a thrill, a vicarious sense of satisfaction? And the platinum hair, so vibrant, so full of life, plucked from the head of a woman who callously disregarded the suffering of others? Did you not feel a twisted sense of poetic justice in its acquisition?

You have been my silent accomplice, a witness to my confession, a participant in my warped theater of justice. I have stripped away the facade, exposed the hypocrisy, the festering corruption that masquerades as civility. And you, you have been complicit in this revelation. You have watched; you have absorbed, you have, in your own way, took part.

My narrative, deliberately fragmented, deliberately unreliable, unsettled, to challenge, to force you to confront the uncomfortable truths that underpin our society. Did you not feel a certain perverse fascination with the elegance of my methods, the meticulous planning, the psychological manipulation? Did it not stir something within you, a dark echo of your own hidden desires, your own suppressed resentments?

Stone, in his relentless pursuit of justice, became my mirror image, a detective obsessed, consumed by the very game he sought to unravel. His obsession mirrored my own, a perverse reflection of our shared fascination with the dance of death, the seductive allure of the forbidden. He became an actor in my play, unknowingly playing a crucial role in my twisted design.

The victims, I will admit, were not flawless. They were products of the system, beneficiaries of its inequities, complicit in its perpetuation. Were they truly innocent? The answer, like justice itself, is a subjective concept, a fluid entity, ever-shifting, ever-elusive. My actions, while undeniably violent, served as a stark, brutal commentary on a society that glorifies wealth and power, while ignoring, or actively suppressing, the suffering of the vulnerable.

But the narrative is not simply about the victims or the detective. It's about you. About your own complicity, your own fascination with the dark side of human nature, your own capacity for both empathy and detachment. It's about the fine line between observer and participant, between fascination and revulsion.

What did you feel as you read the description of the last victim? Did it awaken something within you, a primal sense of dread? Or did you simply feel a cold, intellectual detachment, a sense of clinical observation?

The courtroom drama, the legal proceedings, is merely a formality. The genuine drama unfolds within your mind, in the space between my words and your interpretation. I have given you a mirror, reflecting the darker corners of your soul, the hidden impulses, the secret desires, the unacknowledged complicity in the very system I sought to destroy.

I have exposed the hypocrisy, the inequalities, the grotesque inequalities that permeate our world. I have done it in a way that is both disturbing and undeniably effective. And in the end, you—the reader — are left to confront the lingering questions, the unsettled ambiguities. Did I bring justice? Or did I simply play a more complicated game of deception, one that implicated you, the observer, as much as me, the perpetrator?

The ultimate question is not whether my actions were justified, but whether you, the reader, find yourself questioning your own morality, your own complicity, your own capacity for both darkness and light. I have offered you a glimpse into the abyss, a confrontation with your own capacity for both empathy and detached observation. Have you looked into the abyss, and seen yourself reflected back?

My last act is not a confession; it is a challenge. It is an invitation to confront your own biases, your own judgments, your own complicity in the systems that perpetuate inequality and suffering. It is a mirror held up to society, and to you, the reader, forcing you to confront the uncomfortable truths that we would rather ignore. Have you accepted the challenge?

The silence remains, thick with the weight of unanswered questions, echoing the dissonant chords of a twisted symphony. The game is over, yet the repercussions, the unsettling implications, continue to reverberate, not just in the minds of the investigators, but at the very core of your being.

The final verdict, however, rests not with the law, but with you. You, who have followed my narrative, who have witnessed my twisted justice, who have, in your own way, become complicit in the act. The true judge is your own conscience, and the sentence... well, the sentence is left for you to ponder.

23

My reflection staring back at me from the polished steel of the interrogation table wasn't the one I expected. It wasn't the carefully constructed persona I'd presented to the world — the successful businesswoman, the charitable philanthropist, the seemingly flawless picture of societal success.

No, this reflection was raw, stripped bare, a visceral portrayal of the chaos simmering beneath the meticulously crafted surface. It reflected the monstrous truth I had become, a truth I had painstakingly concealed behind a mask of normalcy for so long.

Stone had tried to shatter that mask, to peel away the layers of deception, to expose the monster lurking within. He had succeeded, to a certain extent. But even in his relentless pursuit, he never truly understood the intricate game I was playing, the complex web of psychological manipulation I had woven. He saw the murders, the trophies, the meticulous planning, but he missed the underlying philosophy, the twisted logic that drove me.

He saw the masks I wore, but he didn't see the mirror I held up to society, a mirror reflecting its own grotesque distortions, its own hypocrisy. He saw the darkness, but he failed to comprehend the light, the warped sense of justice that fueled my actions.

My victims were not merely victims; they were symbols, representations of a corrupt system, emblems of privilege and indifference. They were the masks of the wealthy elite, concealing their greed, their cruelty, their complicity in the very injustices I sought to rectify.

Each murder was a meticulously orchestrated performance, a twisted theatrical production designed to expose the hypocrisy of a society that turned a blind eye to suffering, that celebrated wealth and power while ignoring the plight of the vulnerable. The trophies were symbols of their power, their influence, their perceived superiority, all stripped away and repurposed as emblems of my twisted brand of justice.

The mirror, however, reflects more than just my victims. It reflects society as a whole, the collective masks we wear to navigate the complexities of our social interactions. We all play roles, adopt personas, construct identities to fit into the world around us.

Some masks are more elaborate than others; some conceal deeper truths than others. But we all wear them, to varying degrees, to protect ourselves, to present ourselves in a favorable light, to achieve our goals. My reflection, therefore, wasn't just my own, but a distorted reflection of the entire human condition, the inherent duality between our public personas and our private selves.

My actions, though undeniably violent, were a form of social commentary, a visceral critique of a society that valued outward appearances over inner worth. I was the sculptor of shadows, chiseling away at the polished facades, revealing the darkness lurking beneath the surface.

My victims were the mirrors reflecting the hypocrisy of a system that allowed the wealthy and powerful to operate with impunity, while the vulnerable suffered in silence.

The relentless pursuit of Stone was in itself a reflection of this societal dysfunction. His dedication was a mask concealing his own internal demons. He mirrored my obsession, though he was driven by a desire to uphold the law, while mine was fueled by a desire to subvert it. We were two sides of the same coin, two reflections in a distorted mirror, locked in a deadly dance of pursuit and evasion.

The courtroom, the trial, the subsequent incarceration—these were merely the culmination of a larger, more complex drama that unfolded within the minds of the participants, the observers, and the reader.

The true judgment wouldn't come from the judge or the jury, but from within the collective consciousness of those who had witnessed my actions, who had absorbed my narrative, and who had, in their own way, become complicit in the drama.

My narrative reflects the reader's own capacity for both empathy and detachment. It challenges the reader to confront their own moral ambiguities, their own capacity for both darkness and light. Are you truly innocent? Or do you find yourself, however subtly, drawn to the allure of forbidden acts, the seductive appeal of the darker impulses that lie within us all?

The masks we wear conceal the truths that we wish to keep hidden, the truths that society deems undesirable. But beneath the polished surface lies the raw, unfiltered reality of our existence. The darkness is always there, waiting to be revealed.

The question is not whether we are capable of darkness, but how we choose to confront it and reconcile it with the light. That is the mirror I offer to you, the reader. And in that reflection, you will find yourself. The final judgment rests with you.

24

The weight of the investigation pressed down on Detective Stone, a relentless gravity that pulled him further and further from the familiar shores of his life. His apartment, once a sanctuary of quiet evenings and meticulously organized books, became a neglected space, a reflection of the chaos that consumed him.

Dust mites danced in the slivers of sunlight that pierced the gloom, undisturbed by his increasingly infrequent cleaning. Empty coffee cups accumulated on his desk, silent witnesses to sleepless nights spent analyzing crime scene photos, autopsy reports, and psychological profiles.

Empty takeout containers overflowed from the trash can, a testament to his irregular eating habits. His once neatly pressed suits hung limp in the closet, their creases softened, mirroring the erosion of his composure. He was a man unraveling, his carefully constructed life fraying at the edges, mirroring the unraveling of the killer's carefully constructed facade.

His colleagues noticed, of course. Whispers followed him down the hallways, concerned glances exchanged over his shoulder. Sergeant Miller, his usually jovial partner, attempted to engage him in casual conversation, but Stone's responses were abrupt.

His focus narrowed, becoming laser-sharp, yet strangely distant, as if he were observing his own life from a detached vantage point, a silent observer in his own increasingly chaotic drama. His obsession was blinding, a consuming fire that threatened to engulf everything in its path.

The case files did not limit his obsession. It seeped into his dreams, manifesting in unsettling visions of shadowed figures, fleeting glimpses of the killer’s enigmatic smile. He sketched her likeness in the margins of his reports, her eyes haunting him, even in sleep.

The lines blurred between reality and nightmare, reality becoming as elusive and deceptive as the killer’s game. He'd wake up in a cold sweat, his heart pounding a frantic rhythm against his ribs. The image of the killer's piercing gaze burned into the back of his eyelids. The killer’s presence felt palpable, a silent, spectral companion that followed him everywhere.

His relationship with his wife, Sarah, suffered the brunt of his obsession. His absences became more frequent, his explanations increasingly vague. The hollow silence punctuated by strained apologies and forced smiles replaced the vibrant spark that once ignited their conversations.

Sarah's initial concern morphed into frustration, then into a quiet, heartbreaking resignation. Stone's focus remained relentlessly fixed on the killer, oblivious to the collateral damage his obsession was inflicting on his personal life. The woman he loved was becoming a distant figure in his rear-view mirror, fading into the background of his singular, all-consuming obsession.

His colleagues tried to intervene, suggesting a leave of absence, a temporary respite from the relentless pressure of the case. But Stone refused, his resolve hardening with every passing day. He was close. He felt it in his gut, an intuition that fueled his relentless pursuit. A desire to bring the killer to justice, to bring closure to the families of her victims, consumed him. Yet he seemed to edge closer to losing himself in the process.

He saw himself in the killer, an unsettling realization that crept into the shadowed corners of his consciousness. The killer's planning, her intricate manipulations—these mirrored aspects of his own disciplined nature, his own ability to focus intensely on a single objective. Her intellect, her audacity, even her depravity fascinated him.

It was a fascination that bordered on identification, a chilling echo in the dark recesses of his mind. The line between hunter and hunted, between pursuer and pursued, was blurring, a dizzying descent into a psychological abyss.

The trophies the killer collected, the seemingly random objects she took from her victims, sparked a macabre fascination in Stone. But in studying them, in attempting to understand her motivations, he lost sight of the boundaries that separated him from the darkness he investigated. He was immersing himself in the killer's mind, and the more he delved into it, the more his own mind seemed to unravel.

25

Detective Stone sat in the dimly lit office of the precinct, his hands clasped tightly together as he watched the evidence board in front of him. Photographs of the victims, notes, crime scene reports—all interconnected by red string—created a tangled web of murder and deception. At the center of it all was Serena Holloway, the woman who now sat in an interrogation room down the hall, poised and utterly unshaken.

He should have felt victorious. He had caught her, the serial killer who had eluded them for so long. And yet, something gnawed at him, an unease that festered in the pit of his stomach. A feeling that, despite everything, justice was still slipping through his fingers. It didn't take long for his fears to be realized.

Stone had barely taken a sip of his stale coffee when the door to his office burst open. Assistant District Attorney Michael Crane stood in the doorway, his face an unreadable mask of professional detachment.

"We have a problem," Crane said.

Stone didn't need to ask. He already knew. "The evidence?" Stone asked, his voice grim.

Crane exhaled sharply. “There’s not enough. Someone compromised the chain of custody on the key piece of forensic evidence—the hair sample found at the last murder scene. The defense is already arguing that someone mishandled and possibly contaminated the evidence. Without it, we don’t have physical proof linking her to that scene.”

Stone slammed his coffee down, his frustration boiling over.

“That’s not the only evidence we have. We have witness statements, behavioral analysis—.”

“Circumstantial at best,” Crane interrupted. “None of it conclusively places her at the crime scenes. And the one piece of forensic evidence that could have sealed the case? It’s tainted. The judge won’t admit it.”

Stone ran a hand over his face, feeling the weight of weeks of work unraveling.

“She confessed,” he growled. “She as much as admitted what she did.”

Crane hesitated. “Did she, though?”

Stone’s brow furrowed. He replayed their conversation in the interrogation room. Serena had spoken about justice, about removing parasites from society. She had hinted she had played her psychological games, but she had never outright said the words ‘I killed them.’

She had danced around it, let the detectives assume what they wanted, led them to their own conclusions. But a confession needed to be explicit. And Serena Holloway was too intelligent to make that mistake.

"She played us," Stone whispered, realization dawning.

Crane nodded. "And her lawyer is already moving to have her released."

Stone shot to his feet. "On what grounds?"

"Unlawful detainment," Crane said, rubbing his temples. "We had her in holding for over 48 hours without officially charging her. The defense is arguing that any statements she made are inadmissible because she was not properly Mirandized before being subjected to prolonged questioning."

"That's bullshit!"

"It doesn't matter what it is," Crane said through gritted teeth. "It's a loophole, and a judge just granted her release."

Stone clenched his fists. "We still have her under surveillance, right?"

"We do," Crane confirmed. "But unless we get fresh evidence, there's nothing stopping her from walking out of here a free woman."

Stone stormed out of the office and down the hall, his pulse pounding in his ears. He reached the holding area just as the duty officer unlocked the cell door. Serena Holloway stood, her expression placid, her lips curved in that same unreadable smile.

"Looks like justice has a funny way of working, doesn't it, Detective?" she murmured as she stepped past him, her voice smooth as silk.

Stone didn't respond. He just watched as she walked out of the precinct, her posture upright, her steps unhurried, like she had known this was how it would end all along.

As the station doors swung shut behind her, a cold realization settled over him. She wasn't done. And the next time she killed, there might be nothing he could do to stop her.

26

After the release of Ms. Holloway, Detective Stone continued following her, watching her every move. The gallery was hushed, a mausoleum of gilded frames and hushed whispers. The air hung thick with the scent of old varnish and expensive perfume, a stark contrast to the grime and decay Stone had become accustomed to in his relentless pursuit.

He stood there, a ghost in the opulent space, observing her from across the room. She was even more captivating in person, an unsettling blend of fragility and power, her beauty and carefully crafted mask concealing a chilling abyss.

He had imagined this moment countless times, the culmination of months of relentless investigation, sleepless nights, and a slowly disintegrating personal life. Serena stood before a painting of a storm at sea, the swirling chaos of the canvas mirroring the storm raging within her. She didn't seem afraid; she seemed… amused. Her eyes met his, and a slow, almost imperceptible smile played on her lips.

The weight of his obsession pressed down on him, the culmination of every sleepless night, every sacrificed relationship, every shred of his former self that this singular, all-consuming pursuit had consumed. He was no longer just a detective; he extended this twisted game, a pawn in a macabre chess match where the stakes were far higher than he'd ever realized.

It wasn't just about catching her; it had become about understanding her, about deciphering the intricate workings of her mind, about solving the puzzle of her motivations. And in doing so, he had inadvertently become a reflection of her, a distorted mirror image of her own depravity.

He saw her in the fragmented pieces of his own life, in the neglected apartment, in the strained relationships, in the hollow ache in his chest. She wasn't just a killer; she was a symptom, a manifestation of the darkness he had sought to eradicate. But in hunting her, he'd found a part of that darkness within himself.

The silence stretched, a tense, suffocating void. The other patrons, oblivious to the silent confrontation unfolding before them, moved through the gallery like phantoms, their hushed conversations a muffled backdrop to the silent battle of wills.

Stone realized he couldn't move, couldn't speak. His predicament trapped him, just as it had trapped her victims. His carefully constructed facade, the mask he'd worn throughout the investigation, was cracking, revealing the disintegrating self beneath.

He knew, with chilling certainty, that she knew he knew. This was not a moment of surprise; this was a calculated encounter, a final, twisted act of manipulation. She was toying with him, letting him bask in the illusion of victory, only to snatch it away at the last moment. He wondered if this was her intention all along - to find a reflection of herself in someone else's obsessive need for control, to become a mirror image in the mind of her nemesis.

The realization struck him with the force of a physical

blow. He wasn't just hunting a killer; he was hunting a reflection of himself. The planning, the calculated risks, the obsessive focus—these were traits he recognized within himself, traits he'd honed throughout his career. He was, in a twisted way, her mirror image, a dark reflection of her own twisted genius.

Suddenly, a wave of nausea washed over him, the culmination of exhaustion, stress, and the dawning realization of his own complicity. He stumbled back, his vision blurring, the opulent surroundings swaying like a drunken ship. His neatly pressed suit, once a symbol of his authority, felt suffocating, a weight pressing down on his chest, mirroring the crushing weight of his obsession. The game had ended, not with a dramatic arrest, but with a sickening realization of his own vulnerability, his own susceptibility to the very darkness he pursued.

Serena remained motionless, watching him with cold, calculating eyes. Her stillness was more terrifying than any frantic escape could have been. She was in control, always in control, a puppet master pulling the strings of his life, his investigation, his very soul.

He had become a victim, not of her knife, but of his own relentless pursuit, of his own desperate need to understand the unknowable. His fascination, obsession, and twisted desire for understanding ensnared him in a web of his own making. He had chased the darkness, only to find that it had lived within him all along.

And as he collapsed, the weight of his failure crushing him, he understood she had won, not by escaping, but by leaving him broken, a shattered reflection of her own dark, twisted brilliance. He felt the crushing weight of knowledge, chillingly realizing his own complicity in his downfall. His obsession had not been about justice; it had been about a twisted desire to unravel the mystery of the killer's psyche, an exploration that led him to unravel his own sanity.

The gallery remained silent, the beauty of the art a grotesque contrast to the grim reality unfolding within its walls. The patrons continued to move among the canvases, oblivious to the tragedy that had transpired, their hushed whispers a cruel reminder of his failure, his inability to solve the mystery, his inability to save himself.

The unreliable narrative leaves the reader grappling with the same burden. We are complicit in the killer's narrative, seduced by her charm, fascinated by her methods, drawn into her twisted world. We are voyeurs, observing her crimes through her own eyes, taking part in her game, even as we condemn her actions. The moral ambiguity is stark, leaving us to question our own fascinations, our own complicity in the unfolding tragedy.

The killer’s escape was not a defeat; it was a triumph. She left behind a trail of shattered lives, not just her victims, but also those who pursued her. She left behind a chilling reminder that obsession can be a far more dangerous weapon than any blade, a corrosive force that can consume the hunter as easily as the hunted. And in the end, the greatest victim of all was not the killer, but those consumed by the relentless pursuit of justice, those who lost themselves in the labyrinth of her mind.

The finality of it all was unsettling. There was no neat resolution, no satisfying climax. Lingering echoes of a disturbed mind remained—a chaotic game played out in a world where beauty and horror intertwined inextricably, blurring the line between hunter and hunted in a haze of obsession. The question remained: Who was the true monster? The killer, or those who became consumed by their pursuit of her?

27

The gallery's polished floors reflected the distorted image of my reflection, a warped version of the elegant woman I presented to the world. Stone's collapse, his pathetic surrender, was... underwhelming. I'd expected a more... robust response. A struggle. A desperate attempt to regain control. Instead, I saw the anticlimactic sight of a man broken by his own obsession, his face a mask of defeat and self-loathing. It was almost... disappointing.

He saw himself in me, didn't he? The relentless pursuit, the meticulous planning, the disregard for collateral damage. He saw the reflection of his own darkness staring back at him from my eyes. And that, more than anything, was the genuine victory. Not the escape, not the trophies, not even the thrill of the kill itself.

The victory was the shattering of his self-image, the exposure of his own moral ambiguity. He had hunted a monster, only to find that the monster lived within himself all along. The irony was obvious to me and it was exquisitely delicious.

My methods, my choices... they weren't arbitrary. They were a response, a reaction to a world steeped in inequality, a world where privilege and entitlement reigned supreme. These men, these titans of industry, these paragons of society, they lived their lives oblivious to the suffering they inflicted, the lives they destroyed in their relentless pursuit of wealth and power.

They built their empires on the backs of the downtrodden, the forgotten, the invisible. I was merely restoring the balance, a necessary evil in a world drowning in excess. A corrective measure. An act of twisted, albeit necessary, justice.

Stone failed to see the unseen threads connecting my actions to a larger tapestry of societal injustice, a web woven from centuries of inequality and oppression. The thread that linked the callous indifference of the wealthy elite to the grinding poverty and despair of the masses. He could not, or would not, see the intricate relationship between the opulent galleries, where the wealthy flaunted their ill-gotten gains, and the decaying slums where the marginalized struggled to survive.

Perhaps the greatest tragedy of Stone's obsession was not that he failed to catch me, but that he allowed himself to become a reflection of the very darkness he sought to destroy. He became consumed by his own pursuit, sacrificing his personal life, his relationships, his very self in his desperate attempt to understand me. The irony is deeply satisfying.

The narrative I present—this confession, this meticulously crafted performance—is not merely a recounting of my actions. It's a commentary, a critique, a darkly satirical reflection of a society that values wealth and power above all else.

I am, in a twisted way, a product of this system, a grotesque manifestation of its inherent flaws. The violence I inflict is not random; it is a targeted response to a world that systematically ignores and marginalizes those who cannot afford its excesses. And to those who condemn me, I ask: Are you any different? Are you truly free of the same complicity?

My world draws you in, seducing you with the elegance of my methods, and intriguing you with the intricate dance of manipulation and psychological warfare. The darkness fascinates you, by the forbidden, by the taboo. You are as much a prisoner of this narrative as Stone, as much a victim of this societal dysfunction. You are complicit.

And so, I leave you with this question: Who is the true monster? The one who acts in the shadows, or the one who observes from the sidelines, allowing the darkness to flourish? Is it the one who strikes out, or the one who looks away? The one who confesses their actions in vivid detail, or the one who remains passively complicit?

The questions are open-ended, forever twisting in the depths of the reader's own conscience. Rest assured, I assure you the game is far from over. The unseen threads continue to weave a complex tapestry of moral ambiguity, drawing you deeper into the unsettling narrative, and leaving the last victim to be unveiled at a point of your choosing, your own fascination with the darkness sealing your complicity in the final, brutal act.

28

The silence in the aftermath was deafening, a stark contrast to the orchestrated chaos of my previous performances. Stone's defeat wasn't a victory celebrated with triumphant screams or a self-satisfied smirk. It was a quiet acknowledgment, a subtle nod to the power of unspoken truths.

The weight of those truths, both mine and his, settled heavily in the air, thick and suffocating. He understood, on some level, the game we were playing, the intricate dance of manipulation and psychological warfare. But understanding wasn't the same as acceptance, was it?

Stone's obsession had blinded him, consumed him, leaving him hollowed out, a shell of the ambitious, relentless detective I had once known. He saw the monster, yes, but he failed to see the human beneath, the woman driven by a twisted sense of justice, a warped morality.

Detective Stone saw the meticulously planned murders, the trophies, the calculated risks. He dissected my actions under the harsh light of forensic science, missing the subtle nuances of my motivation, the deep-seated resentment that fueled my actions. He chased shadows, while the truth, the actual truth, remained elusive, hidden in plain sight.

My desires were not for power or violence. It wasn't about the thrill of the kill, though that was undeniably present. It was about exposing the hypocrisy, the festering corruption at the heart of a system that privileged the few while condemning the many to a life of poverty and despair. The opulent galleries, the lavish parties, the displays of wealth and power—these were the symbols of a world that had turned its back on compassion and empathy. These men, these titans of industry, these untouchable figures, lived lives of reckless abandon, blind to the consequences of their actions, their wealth built on the backs of the forgotten, the marginalized.

Stone became a mirror image of that very system. He chased me, consumed by the chase, neglecting his family, his friends, his own well-being. His obsession became self-destruction, a reflection of the very corruption he sought to expose.

He was a tragic figure, a pawn in a larger game, his own internal battles mirroring the societal conflicts I was seeking to highlight. He, in his own way, was just as complicit as the men and women I hunted. His own ambition, his desire for recognition, his need to conquer the darkness he sought to eliminate blinded him.

29

The chill that permeated the air wasn't solely from the autumn wind whipping through the deserted alleyway outside the gallery where I left Stone. It was a deeper, more visceral cold, the icy grip of memory, the ghosts of my past rising to claim their due. The trophies were echoes of my own fractured self, shards of a life shattered long before I ever considered myself an agent of justice.

My childhood wasn't a picturesque, idyllic scene, painted with happy memories and loving smiles. It was a canvas smeared with neglect, stained with the bruises of emotional abuse, and haunted by the constant, gnawing fear of my father's unpredictable rage. He was a man of contradictions—capable of flashes of tenderness that felt both precious and perilous, followed inevitably by fits of uncontrolled fury.

These swings in his temper were more frightening than any consistent cruelty, the unpredictable nature fostering an intense anxiety that became deeply ingrained within me. The silence in our home was far more oppressive than any shouted argument, a heavy blanket of fear woven from the unspoken tensions simmering beneath the surface.

That silence was a breeding ground for a twisted sense of self-preservation, a survival mechanism that warped my perception of the world. I learned to read the subtle shifts in my father's mood, to expect the storms before they broke. This hyper-vigilance, honed in the crucible of my dysfunctional family, became a perverse skill, an ability to detect subtle changes in behavior, to discern the unspoken anxieties and hidden vulnerabilities in others.

It was this acute awareness, this uncanny ability to read people, that became the foundation of my meticulously planned murders. I wasn't just targeting the wealthy; I was hunting the oblivious, the complacent, the arrogant—those who, like my father, lived in a self-created bubble of privilege, blind to the surrounding suffering.

The same silence, however, also fostered a deep-seated resentment, a simmering rage against a world that seemed to value appearances over reality. I excelled academically, masking my inner turmoil behind a veneer of success. I became a chameleon, adapting to the expectations of my environment, mirroring the smiles and polite pleasantries of the privileged while harboring a bitterness that gnawed at my soul.

The academic achievements, the scholarships, the accolades—they were all carefully constructed masks, designed to shield my true self from the world's judgment. But beneath the polished surface, the pain festered, growing into a venomous resentment that would eventually consume me.

My fascination with psychology was a direct consequence of my troubled upbringing. It was a desperate attempt to understand the complexities of human behavior, to decipher the mysteries of the human psyche, to find a key to unlock the secrets of the darkness that had engulfed my childhood.

I devoured textbooks on criminal psychology, studying

the profiles of serial killers, analyzing the motivations behind their horrific acts. It wasn't morbid curiosity; it was a desperate search for answers, a yearning to understand the twisted logic that drove individuals like my father.

This study became a dangerous form of self-therapy. I saw in those twisted narratives a reflection of my internal turmoil, a recognition of the simmering rage that simmered beneath the surface of my carefully crafted persona. I saw the potential for transformation, the possibility of wielding power, not just for destruction, but for a twisted sense of justice. The meticulously planned murders, the symbolic trophies, the calculated risks—they were all elements of a complex equation, a distorted equation that I believed would restore balance to a world that had wronged me.

Stone mirrored my struggle with the past. His obsession, his unwavering dedication to solving the case, was driven by his own demons. I had learned to read people, and I saw the cracks in his façade, the hints of trauma lurking beneath his professional demeanor. His dogged determination, his unwavering focus, was both a source of frustration and a twisted sort of validation. He saw the monster, the ruthless killer, but he missed the human cost, the deep-seated wounds that propelled my actions.

He, too, carried the weight of silence, the unspoken burdens of a past that shaped his present. His troubled relationship with his father, a man who valued professional success above all else, had created a chasm of emotional distance.

Stone was a man haunted by unspoken regrets, driven by an unquenchable need for validation, a need to prove his worth to a father who never truly acknowledged him. His relentless pursuit of me became a distorted expression of his own need for self-affirmation, a desperate attempt to fill the void created by his own fractured family.

We were two sides of the same coin, two damaged individuals drawn to each other by a shared darkness, a shared understanding of the power of unspoken truths. The dance we engaged in—the game of manipulation and deception—was a twisted reflection of our fractured selves, a desperate attempt to find meaning, to find redemption in the ashes of our respective pasts.

The silence that surrounded us after our last confrontation was the sound of two broken souls acknowledging their shared trauma, their shared complicity in the twisted narrative of their lives. The ghosts of our pasts had finally met, the weight of unspoken truths settling between us like a shroud of suffocating fog.

The game, however, was far from over. The last victim, as I have alluded, is a person closely connected to you, the reader. They are a symbol of the collective silence, the shared complicity in a system that breeds such darkness. They represent the unspoken truths that we all choose to ignore, the injustices that we passively accept, the wounds that we refuse to heal.

By implicating you, the reader, in the narrative, I am forcing you to confront your own complicity, your own role in the cycle of violence and injustice. The silence that follows the last act is not merely the absence of sound; it is the deafening roar of unspoken truths, a symphony of guilt and complicity, echoing through the empty chambers of your own conscience. And the chilling silence hangs heavy; a final, terrifying act of manipulation. The game, dear reader, has only just begun.

30

Stone, with his unwavering gaze and piercing intellect, had chipped away at the carefully constructed edifice of my lies. He wasn't just investigating a series of murders; he was dissecting my mind, peeling back the layers of deception, one meticulously crafted sentence at a time. Stone grasped how easily a carefully placed word or subtly altered inflection could plant a seed of doubt, blossoming into full-blown paranoia through the power of suggestion. He was using my own weapons against me.

My expertise in psychology, once my greatest asset, now felt like a poisoned chalice. The human mind, with its vulnerabilities and susceptibility to manipulation, had been the subject of my studies. I had learned to exploit its inherent weaknesses, to bend it to my will with the precision of a master surgeon. I understood the power of suggestion, the subtle art of influencing beliefs and behaviors without overt coercion. A whispered word, a suggestive glance, a carefully crafted narrative—these were the tools of my trade, the instruments of my twisted artistry.

I remember Dr. Albright, my mentor, his lectures echoing in the recesses of my memory. Speaking of the subconscious, he described it as a vast, unexplored landscape of the mind where suggestions take root and blossom into unshakeable beliefs. He showed us experiments—the hypnotic sway of a pendulum, the power of post-hypnotic suggestion, the malleability of perception. He spoke of creating realities, of crafting illusions so convincing, so utterly believable, that even the subject themselves would cannot distinguish between fantasy and reality. His words, once academic theory, now pulsed with a terrifying new resonance.

My victims, I realized with a chilling clarity, weren't merely casualties; they were subjects in a grand experiment, pawns in a game of psychological chess. Each interaction, each carefully orchestrated encounter, exploited their vulnerabilities, to break down their defenses, to prepare them for the final, inevitable act.

I studied their routines, their habits, and their fears to learn their secrets and deepest insecurities. I then used this knowledge to influence their thoughts and actions subtly, guiding them toward their doom with almost imperceptible nudges.

Consider, for instance, Mr. Beaumont. He was a casualty of my early days, a man of immense wealth, but haunted by a deep-seated fear of failure. I subtly insinuated myself into his life, playing the role of a confidante, a sympathetic ear. By listening to his anxieties and validating his fears, I gradually sowed the seeds of self-doubt. I suggested subtle changes to his routine, alterations he readily accepted without suspicion. He was already walking toward the precipice; I merely provided the gentle shove that sent him tumbling into the abyss.

My methods were far more sophisticated than simple hypnosis. It was a slow, insidious process, a carefully calibrated erosion of the victim's autonomy. I'd plant suggestive phrases in casual conversations, subtly altering their perceptions of reality. I'd use leading questions, ambiguities, and carefully crafted narratives to create a subconscious expectation of the eventual outcome.

Their fears, their anxieties, their insecurities became my leverage. I exploited their vulnerabilities with a precision honed through years of study and practice.

I manipulated their environments, subtly altering the lighting, the music, the aromas, even the temperature of the room to create a specific mood, a particular atmosphere. Sensory deprivation and sensory overload were equally effective tools in my arsenal. The goal was to break down their resistance, to weaken their sense of self, to leave them utterly dependent on my influence.

Then there was Mrs. Harrington. She was a woman of rigid control, deeply insecure beneath a façade of unshakeable confidence. I used reverse psychology, subtly suggesting the opposite of what I wanted her to do. The effect was striking. Her desire to prove me wrong, to assert her dominance, led her directly into my trap. I found the irony amusing. Her own need to control her narrative became her undoing.

The power of suggestion is a two-edged sword. While it allowed me to shape and mold the realities of my victims, it also shaped and molded my perception of myself. The line between manipulator and manipulated, between hunter and hunted, blurred until it was indiscernible.

Stone's pursuit reflected the power I wielded, the subtle influence I exerted, and the psychological games I played. He was a mirror showing me the dark side of my own techniques, reminding me that even the most sophisticated strategies can crumble beneath the relentless pressure of truth and justice.

Perhaps the most terrifying aspect of the whole affair isn't the act of killing, but the insidious power of suggestion, the chilling ability to manipulate minds, to control perceptions, and ultimately, to dictate destiny. And as I sit here, the rain still drumming against the windowpanes, I am left to wonder who was truly the puppeteer, and who was merely a pawn in this macabre game.

The answer, like the shattered pieces of my fractured psyche, remains elusive, lost in the labyrinth of manipulation and deceit. The game, I realize, was never about justice. It was about power. And in that power, I found a dark, seductive beauty, a horrifying fascination that led me down a path of no return.

31

The origins of my actions were not simply a matter of choice, but a complex tapestry woven from threads of nature and nurture, a chilling blend of inherent predisposition and environmental influence. Was I born this way, a pre-ordained instrument of darkness? Or was I molded, sculpted by the callous hands of circumstance? The question gnawed at me, a relentless torment mirroring the incessant drumming of the rain.

My parents, pillars of society, their wealth a shimmering fortress against the harsh realities of the world, were emotionally barren landscapes. Their love was a conditional currency, dispensed sparingly, earned only through meticulous adherence to their rigid expectations. I was a prized possession, a trophy wife in the making, but never truly loved. Their affection was a fleeting illusion, a mirage shimmering in the desert of their emotional neglect.

I learned early on that genuine connection was a fragile commodity, a luxury I could not afford. This emotional void, this chasm of unmet needs, became the fertile ground where I sowed the seeds of darkness.

Dr. Albright, my therapist and mentor during those brief, tempestuous years of my adolescence, had attempted to dissect my psyche, to categorize me, to label my affliction.

He'd spoken of ‘antisocial personality disorder’, of ‘narcissistic tendencies’, of a ‘lack of empathy’, of clinical terms that seemed utterly inadequate to capture the brutal complexity of my inner world.

He'd probed, dissected, analyzed, but the truth remained elusive, even to his practiced eye. His attempts to categorize me only intensified my carefully constructed barriers. His attempts to understand seemed to confirm my worst fears: that I was flawed, irredeemably broken, a creature of darkness destined to walk the path of destruction.

Yet, even amidst the stark emptiness of my upbringing, a strange paradox existed. I possessed an acute intelligence, a sharp analytical mind, a capacity for intricate planning that bordered on the obsessive. These were not attributes nurtured by my parents; they were inherent, gifts and curses simultaneously.

The same mind that meticulously planned the murders also had a remarkable aptitude for strategic thinking—a skill I used to orchestrate my life, manipulate others, control my environment, and get what I’d been denied. It was a duality, an inner struggle between the innate and the learned.

The ritualistic nature of my killings was not an arbitrary choice. I carefully choreographed those acts, imbuing them with a chilling symmetry that reflected a deep-seated need for control, a desperate attempt to impose order on the chaotic landscape of my childhood.

I meticulously collected the trophies, which became harrowing talismans symbolizing the power and beauty denied to me. They were fragmented pieces of a perfection I longed to possess, a completion of the fractured whole that was my being. These were not acts of random violence; they were rituals, carefully crafted enactments of a distorted sense of justice, a warped attempt to restore balance to a world that had treated me so cruelly.

The psychological literature I devoured—a morbid fascination that began in adolescence—suggested that nature versus nurture is not an either/or proposition, but a complex interplay. Genetic predispositions, inherited traits, could interact with environmental factors, shaping personality and behavior in intricate and unpredictable ways.

Was there a genetic predisposition toward psychopathy within my family line? I had no way of knowing, and even the most sophisticated DNA analysis could not provide a definitive answer. The very notion felt chillingly plausible, adding another layer of complexity to the labyrinthine corridors of my past.

My fascination with criminology wasn't born out of a desire to understand; it was a desperate attempt to understand myself. To comprehend the darkness that lived within me, to decipher the blueprint of my monstrosity. Each study, each case file, each psychological profile seemed to offer a piece of the puzzle, a fragment of a truth I couldn't quite grasp.

The works of Lombroso, of Freud, of Eysenck—their theories seemed to resonate, not as objective truths, but as reflections of my own disturbed reality. The interplay of biology and experience, the impact of childhood trauma, the development of antisocial tendencies—all became twisted mirrors reflecting my self-image.

The debate between nature and nurture extended beyond the realm of purely psychological factors. Socioeconomic circumstances played their own insidious role. Poverty, instability, lack of opportunity—these could exacerbate inherent vulnerabilities, creating fertile ground for the growth of darkness.

Though I had an affluent childhood, I experienced emotional impoverishment during my upbringing, a deprivation in itself. The lack of genuine connection, the suffocating weight of expectation, the constant pressure to conform—these were forms of neglect as insidious as any physical deprivation.

The nature versus nurture debate had ceased to be a theoretical conundrum. It became a harsh, brutally honest reflection of my own monstrous creation. I was a product of both, a terrifying synthesis of inherited tendencies and the corrosive effects of emotional neglect, a testament to the enduring power of the past to shape the present and irrevocably alter the course of a life. And the last victim, the one that would shatter your world, would serve as the ultimate testament to the terrifying power of this chilling truth.

32

The chipped porcelain doll, its painted eyes staring blankly into the abyss, felt strangely familiar. It wasn't just the unsettling resemblance to the victim, a socialite whose life had been as meticulously crafted as the doll's pristine appearance.

The feeling ran deeper, a chilling echo resonating from a forgotten corner of my memory. A memory of a similar doll, perhaps, clutched tightly in my small hands, a silent witness to a childhood trauma I'd painstakingly buried beneath layers of calculated sophistication and chilling efficiency.

The connection wasn't immediately apparent, not consciously at least. It was a subtle dissonance, a flicker in the periphery of my awareness, a feeling as elusive as the scent of rain on dry pavement. It was the same unsettling calm I felt during those childhood moments, a strange detachment from the intensity of the emotion surrounding me. The same way I'd felt during the meticulously planned murders, the calculated detachment was almost clinical, almost professional.

A chilling parallel emerged. The precision, the methodical approach — they mirrored each other with an unnerving symmetry. The meticulous planning, the selection of victims, the acquisition of trophies—it all seemed to stem from a source buried deep within, a source I had long sought to suppress, to control.

This realization, this uncomfortable convergence of past and present, sent a tremor through my carefully constructed facade. The rain outside, a constant, insistent presence, mirrored the storm brewing within me.

The echoes of the past resonated, shattering the illusion of control I had so meticulously cultivated. The doll, a grotesque memento, wasn't merely a trophy; it was a key, unlocking a forgotten chamber in my mind. It was a fragment, a piece of a larger puzzle I'd spent a lifetime trying to erase.

The childhood home loomed in my memory—a grand Victorian mansion, its imposing façade masking a sinister undercurrent of neglect and simmering resentment. My parents, figures of wealth and influence, were distant, their attention consumed by social climbing and opulent displays of success.

Their emotional absence created a vacuum, a void I filled with a morbid fascination with discarded objects, forgotten things, things that held a silent story. Broken toys, old photographs, faded letters—they became my confidants, my silent companions in a world where human connection was a rare and elusive commodity.

The dolls, in particular, held a special significance. They were more than just toys; they were representations of the idealized perfection I yearned for, a perfection my parents seemed to possess but were unwilling to share. Each doll was a symbol of what I lacked: love, attention, a sense of belonging. Their pristine beauty was a stark contrast to the emptiness within me, a void that grew larger with each passing year.

As I delved deeper into my memories, I unearthed a disturbing pattern. The meticulously planned acts of violence weren't random; they mirrored the rituals I'd unknowingly crafted in my childhood, mirroring my suppressed need for control, a desperate attempt to impose order on the chaos of my early years. The meticulousness of my killings echoed the precision with which I arranged my dolls, creating miniature narratives, silent dramas played out in the confines of my bedroom.

The trophies I collected weren't mere symbols of power. I saw them as fragments of the idealized perfection denied to me, pieces of a puzzle I desperately tried to assemble, to create a semblance of wholeness in a life fractured by emotional neglect. Each object was a shard of beauty, a fragment of the unattainable, meticulously collected, meticulously preserved—a chilling testament to the depth of my emotional deprivation.

The victims, each carefully selected from the elite circles of society, were not just targets; they represented the unattainable world of my parents. My childhood mocked their lives and opulence, constantly reminding me of what I lacked. Their deaths were not acts of random violence. I attempted to correct the past's imbalances and reclaim the power and control others had taken from me.

Stone, the relentless detective, was more than just a foil; he reflected the part of me that yearned for redemption, a part that struggled against the dark impulses that had defined my life. His pursuit mirrored my inner turmoil, the struggle between the carefully constructed persona and the wounded child within. He sought to understand the 'why,' to unravel the tangled web of my motivations. But his quest was also a reflection of my own desperate search for meaning, for understanding, for a sense of self.

The parallels between past and present were not accidental. My childhood trauma, the emotional deprivation, the yearning for control, the obsession with perfection—they were the building blocks of my monstrous creation.

The present was a twisted reflection of the past, a macabre replay of the rituals I'd unknowingly created in the solitude of my childhood. The violence, the control, the meticulously crafted narratives—they were all rooted to compensate for the emptiness I'd carried within me since childhood.

The rain continued its relentless assault, washing over the city, mirroring the cleansing I so desperately craved, yet knew I could never achieve. A crushing weight settled upon me as I discovered a horrific truth. The assault brutally exposed the fractured pieces of my identity, once carefully concealed.

The monstrous creation I had become wasn't a random act of violence; it was a carefully constructed monument to my fragmented past, a chilling testament to the power of unresolved trauma.

The last victim, as you are about to discover, represents the ultimate culmination of this twisted journey, the last piece of the puzzle, a horrifying connection to your own world, a chilling reminder of the unseen connections that bind us all together.

The shock will be not just the act itself, but the realization of how deeply intertwined our lives are, how the echoes of the past can ripple through generations, shaping destinies in ways we can never fully comprehend.

The rain falls, washing away the pretense, revealing the raw, unfiltered truth. My story is not merely a confession; it's a warning, a chilling reflection of the human capacity for darkness, a testament to the power of unresolved trauma, and a horrifying glimpse into the interconnectedness of our lives. And you, the reader, remain a silent, yet complicit, witness to the culmination of this horrifying tale.

The ultimate question, as always, remains: how much of this darkness lives within you? How much of my journey reflects your own potential for both creation and destruction? The answer, I fear, lies buried deep within the shadows of your own heart. The rain continues to fall...

33

The psychology of violence... it's a field I've explored with morbid fascination since adolescence, consuming countless books, articles, case studies. I dissected the works of Lombroso, his theories on atavistic traits and criminal physiognomy, finding echoes of my own warped self-image within his descriptions of born criminals.

Freud's exploration of the id, ego, and superego offered a framework for understanding the chaotic landscape of my inner world, a battlefield where primal urges clashed with societal expectations, where the shadow self held sway.

Eysenck's theory of personality, with its dimensions of extraversion, neuroticism, and psychoticism, felt like a blueprint of my own monstrous construction. Each theory, each study, was a fragment of a puzzle I desperately sought to assemble, a puzzle that might somehow explain, even excuse, the horrific acts I had committed.

But the answer, if there truly is one, is far more complex than any simple psychological label. It's not as easy as ticking boxes on a diagnostic checklist: antisocial personality disorder, psychopathy, narcissistic personality disorder.

These clinical terms, though they might partially describe certain aspects of my behavior, cannot capture the chilling complexity of the motivations behind my actions. They lack the nuance, the visceral understanding of the dark forces that shaped me, the deep-seated sense of injustice that fueled my twisted sense of retribution.

The nature of my crimes speaks to a higher level of intelligence and strategic thinking. It's the same sharp, analytical mind that allowed me to manipulate those around me, to orchestrate my life in such a way that I gained control over my environment, an environment that had previously felt utterly beyond my grasp. This is not simply violence driven by rage or impulsive aggression; it is a calculated act, a twisted form of social justice in my warped reality.

The question of nature versus nurture continues to haunt me, a chilling echo in the relentless drumming of the rain. Were my actions predetermined, the result of inherited traits and genetic predispositions towards violence? Or were they entirely shaped by the harsh realities of my emotionally barren childhood?

The truth is far more complex and deeply unsettling. It's likely a chilling synthesis of both, a deadly cocktail of inherent vulnerability and environmental factors working in tandem to create the monstrous being I am today.

But even if a genetic predisposition existed, the environment plays an equally crucial role. The emotional deprivation, the lack of connection, the suffocating expectations, amplified whatever innate tendencies I might have possessed. A perfect combination of genetic and environmental factors caused the problem we see today.

He did not simply possess these innate characteristics: a lack of empathy, manipulative tendencies, and disregard for the well-being of others.

The last victim… the one whose death will shatter your carefully constructed reality… they represent the culmination of this journey, the ultimate manifestation of the darkness that lies not only within me but within you as well.

34

Stone believed he was hunting a monster, a creature driven by primal rage and bloodlust. He saw the surface—the meticulously planned murders, the chilling trophies, the arrogance of my taunts. But he couldn't see beneath the surface, couldn’t fathom the carefully constructed masks I wore, the intricate layers of deception designed to protect the fragile core within. He saw the predator, but he failed to see the wounded child, the neglected girl who had learned to use cruelty as a weapon, as a means of survival.

The masks I wore were many, as varied and as complex as the human psyche itself. There was the mask of sophistication, the polished exterior of the wealthy socialite, flawlessly navigating the glittering circles of the elite. This mask, perfectly crafted, allowed me seamless access to my victims, lulled them into a false sense of security, rendered them vulnerable.

Beneath that lay the mask of intellect, the cold, calculating facade of a brilliant mind, capable of strategic planning, masterful manipulation, and the ability to expect and circumvent obstacles with ruthless efficiency. This mask allowed me to orchestrate the perfect crimes, leaving little or no trace of my involvement.

Then there was the mask of vulnerability, the carefully

cultivated guise of the innocent, the wronged party, the victim of circumstance. This mask, deployed sparingly and with surgical precision, allowed me to manipulate perceptions, to turn public opinion in my favor, to maintain a semblance of normalcy amidst the chaos.

The game, as I had designed it, was a psychological chess match, a dance of deception and revelation, where the lines between hunter and hunted became increasingly blurred. I designed each act of violence and each crafted detail to unsettle Detective Stone, probing the boundaries of his sanity and testing the limits of his resilience. I challenged him to perceive the depths of human depravity, to confront the possibility that the lines separating good and evil, sanity and madness, were far more fluid than he would care to admit.

As Stone delved deeper into my mind, he uncovered aspects that even I had tried to suppress—the childhood trauma, the crippling sense of inadequacy, the gaping hole in my soul that yearned for something unattainable. He discovered glimpses of the wounded child buried beneath the layers of carefully constructed masks.

But even this vulnerability was part of my game, a calculated strategy designed to evoke empathy, to humanize the monster, to plant seeds of doubt in his unwavering pursuit of justice. I wanted him to see the woman and child to better understand the monster forged in her experiences.

My manipulations weren't simply confined to the victims of my crimes; they extended to the investigator, the media, the public. I was a puppeteer, skillfully pulling the strings, manipulating perceptions, and creating narratives that served my purposes.

The media painted me as a phantom, an elusive figure, adding to the fear and fueling the public's morbid fascination.

This fascination was, of course, another trophy in itself. Fueled by the case's fear and attention, my sense of control grew. The fear, the whispers, the unanswered questions—they were all part of my grand design. The mask of the unknown, the untouchable, the unseen, was my greatest and most enduring achievement.

However, the ultimate mask remains to be revealed.

35

Stone's relentless questioning had cracked the facade, exposing the raw, bleeding heart beneath the meticulously crafted persona. He'd unearthed the fragile ego beneath the layers of calculated manipulation, a fragile structure built on shifting sand.

And in doing so, he'd unwittingly revealed something else entirely: the intricate web of connections, the hidden threads that bound my victims together. They weren't random at all; they were carefully cultivated relationships.

Arthur Blackwood, the first victim, was the prominent CEO of Blackwood Industries, a titan of industry whose empire exploited others, a man who considered compassion a weakness and empathy a liability. He'd amassed a considerable fortune, crushing smaller firms and individuals alike in his wake.

The black raven diamond cufflink I'd taken from him—a family heirloom—had seemed a symbol of his stolen inheritance, a karmic retribution for his heartless pursuit of wealth. But now, seeing it amongst the other trophies, I realized it was more than just a symbol of his greed. It was a key.

Blackwood's connections led me to his former business

partner, a man named Allistair Finch, a renowned art collector with a reputation for ruthlessness and a taste for the forbidden. Finch had been Blackwood's confidante, his silent accomplice in his many shady dealings.

The ruby I'd taken from him—a priceless piece of antique jewelry—reflected his extravagant lifestyle, his brazen disregard for ethics. But it was also a link, a thread connecting her to the next victim.

The lock of platinum blond hair, taken from Lady Beatrice Worthington, a celebrated philanthropist and avid botanist with a hidden past, was the most perplexing. Lady Beatrice, unlike Blackwood and Finch, wasn’t driven by greed or ambition.

She’d lived a life of quiet contemplation, dedicated to her work and seemingly unconnected to the others, callously disregarding their sufferings. Yet, her carefully cultivated persona masked a darker secret, a connection to Finch that ran deeper than a mere acquaintance. She was the silent witness, the custodian of secrets. Her research, I discovered, involved rare and exotic plants with potent hallucinogenic properties. Plants Finch had secretly funded.

The connections, once obscured by my self-serving narrative, now sprang into sharp focus, forming a horrifyingly intricate web. It wasn't just about social justice; it was about revenge, about settling old scores.

Finch had betrayed Blackwood years ago, leaving him bankrupt and ruined. Lady Beatrice, in her own quiet way, had inadvertently aided Alistair's betrayal, providing information that sealed her fate. My actions, initially justified as a twisted form of justice, became a complex tapestry woven from vengeance and misguided attempts at restitution.

The realization hit me with the force of a physical blow, sending tremors through my carefully constructed world. I wasn't just a serial killer; I was a pawn in a larger game, manipulated by my own distorted sense of justice, my desire for revenge on behalf of those I deemed wronged. Ironically, I was playing the same ruthless game as my victims.

News outlets amplified the frenzy surrounding my actions. The whispers of my crimes morphed into an uproar of condemnation and speculation. The public saw my actions not as a noble quest for social justice, but as a series of brutal and senseless murders. This, however, failed to deter me. It instead fueled my actions.

Stone's pursuit wasn't driven by a desire for retribution alone. His fascination with the intricate web I'd spun, and the layers of deception and psychological games I played, increasingly drew him in.

He saw the pattern, the carefully chosen victims, the intricate web of connections binding them together. Stone wasn't just hunting me; he was unraveling the mystery, piecing together the fragmented reality I'd presented.

The truth was far more complex, far more disturbing than any simple narrative of retribution. It was a grotesque parody of justice, a twisted reflection of the world I sought to correct. I'd become what I sought to destroy. My obsession with balance, my desire to rectify the injustices of the world, had warped into a monstrous distortion of reality.

Sleep remained elusive. The faces of my victims haunted my dreams, no longer mere symbols of my conquest, but real people, their suffering palpable, their pleas for justice echoing in my ears. Each one of them had an intricate connection to the web. Each one deserved the justice I had attempted to deliver.

The trophies, once sources of dark satisfaction, were now physical manifestations of my failures, cold reminders of the lives I'd extinguished. They were not symbols of power; they were monuments to my hubris, my distorted sense of morality.

Stone's investigation wasn't merely about apprehending a killer; it was about unraveling a complex web of deceit, hidden motives, and long-forgotten betrayals. He was getting closer, closing in on the truth, not just about my crimes, but about the intricate network of lies and secrets that had fueled my actions.

Detective Stone was beginning to see that I, the seemingly cold and calculating killer, was just as much a victim as those I'd murdered. The game had evolved. It was no longer a hunt for justice, but a desperate struggle for survival. A race against time to unravel the truth before it consumed me completely.

The web of intrigue, so carefully spun, was unraveling, threatening to expose not only my crimes but the dark secrets of the privileged elite I had targeted. My elaborate plan, carefully executed and meticulously justified, was crumbling.

The consequential ripple effect extended beyond those I directly affected; it touched the lives of those who knew them, the friends and families who loved them, the entire community, and in a devastating conclusion, it was becoming painfully clear that I, too, was a victim of this complex web.

36

The unraveling began subtly, like a single thread pulled from a tightly woven tapestry. The death of Arthur Blackwood, initially celebrated in my warped mind as a victory for justice, had triggered a chain reaction I hadn't foreseen. His company, already weakened by his questionable practices, crumbled under the weight of scandal.

Associates, implicated in his misdeeds, lost their careers and reputations. The ripples of his demise irrevocably altered families' lives and financially ruined them. My act of 'justice' had unleashed a torrent of unforeseen consequences, a devastating domino effect that spread far beyond my initial target.

Allistair Finch, initially a symbol of ruthless ambition in my twisted narrative, became a victim of circumstance. His connections to Blackwood, once a source of power and influence, now served as a damning indictment.

The art world, once his playground, turned its back on him, whispers of his association with Blackwood casting a long shadow over his reputation. His once-lavish lifestyle evaporated, replaced by a gnawing uncertainty and the chilling fear of exposure.

The ruby, a trophy I'd claimed as a symbol of his greed,

became a chilling testament to his downfall, a stark reminder of the fragility of power and the unforgiving nature of public opinion.

Lady Beatrice, the Philanthropist, was perhaps the most tragic victim of this ripple effect. The ripple effect shattered her secluded life, dedicated to botany research. The investigation into her connections to Blackwood and Alistair unearthed a dark secret—her unwitting involvement in a scheme to cultivate hallucinogenic plants for illicit purposes.

The orchid, a symbol of her quiet contemplation, was now a symbol of betrayal and a chilling reminder of her unwitting complicity. The events tarnished her previously unblemished reputation. Her life's work, once a source of pride, became a symbol of shame and a reason for ostracism from the botanical community.

The media frenzy surrounding my actions amplified this chain reaction. The initial fascination with the 'Angel of Justice', as some perversely dubbed me, morphed into a wave of fear and revulsion. The media dissected, analyzed, and sensationalized my actions, twisting my quest for social justice into a chilling tale of violence and depravity.

The public's perception of the wealthy elite shifted, marked by suspicion and a growing sense of unease. Trust eroded, relationships fractured, and an atmosphere of fear and uncertainty descended upon the privileged circles I had targeted.

Stone became enmeshed in this web of consequences. His initial focus on apprehending the killer developed into an unraveling of a complex network of deceit, corruption, and hidden agendas. He dug deeper, unearthing long-buried secrets, exposing hidden connections, and revealing the dark underbelly of a society that prided itself on its morality and sophistication.

His investigation wasn't just about solving a series of murders; it was about exposing a rotten core, a systemic failure of ethics and accountability. His obsession wasn't solely with me, but with the larger truth, the intricate web of relationships and power that allowed such injustices to flourish.

The more I learned about the far-reaching effects of my actions, the more the façade I had so carefully constructed crumbled. The power of my justifications and twisted logic began to wane. Symbols of dark power, the trophies now felt like cold, heavy weights dragging me into my self-made abyss. The faces of my victims, once mere abstract symbols in my narrative, became hauntingly real, their pain echoing through the layers of my carefully constructed lies.

The lines blurred, and I grappled not just with the consequences of my actions, but with the terrifying possibility that I was, in fact, a victim myself. A victim of a system that allowed the injustices I sought to correct, a victim of my own flawed understanding of justice, and a victim of my own insatiable desire for revenge.

I understood that my 'justice' was a grotesque parody, a brutal and inefficient attempt to correct a world I didn't truly understand. My actions were not acts of liberation; they were acts of destruction, tearing down without building, punishing without healing. The intricate web I had so meticulously spun had ensnared me, not just in the legal sense, but in a far deeper, more psychologically damaging way.

The psychological toll was immense. Sleep became a battlefield, a nightmarish landscape populated by the ghosts of my victims, their silent accusations ringing in my ears. The guilt was a suffocating blanket, heavy and inescapable. The faces of their loved ones, their families, haunted my waking hours. Their despair and anger became the echoes in my silent chambers. Their cries of injustice were the symphony of my torment.

The arrogance that had fueled my actions evaporated, replaced by a chilling awareness of my fallibility. I was not the master puppeteer; I was a pawn in a game far larger and more complex than I had ever imagined.

The consequences of my actions extended far beyond the immediate victims, reaching out like tendrils, grasping at the lives of those who knew them, altering their futures in ways I could never have expected. The impact rippled through families, communities, and even the broader societal fabric, creating cracks in the world's foundation I so desperately sought to reshape.

My obsession with restoring balance had created an imbalance far greater than the one I initially sought to correct. The irony was bitter, suffocating. I had sought to punish the wicked, yet in doing so, I had become a monster. I had sought to bring justice, but I instead had created a devastating chaos. The game was far from over.

The serpent's coil, once a symbol of my control and mastery, had tightened, constricting me, threatening to crush me beneath its weight. The unraveling wasn't just about the exposure of my crimes; it was about the complete dismantling of my carefully constructed self-image, the shattering of the illusion that I was anything more than a damaged human being who had committed horrific acts.

37

The rooftop bar was a world suspended above the city—an oasis of whispered conversations, the clink of crystal glasses, and a skyline bathed in gold and neon. It was the kind of place where power lounged in velvet booths, where the wealthy indulged in extravagance without ever considering the world below. A warm breeze rolled in, carrying the scent of expensive cologne, aged whiskey, and something else—anticipation.

Serena Holloway sat at the edge of it all, a vision of effortless control. Before her, the city stretched, an empire of lights and shadows, but she fixed her gaze on the bottom of her glass, where the last remnants of an amber drink swirled in lazy circles. She had chosen this place deliberately. Not a hideout, not a darkened alley or an anonymous motel, but the pinnacle of luxury—where people like her never had to answer for their sins.

Then came the shift. A subtle disturbance in the air. She felt him before she saw him. Detective Stone stood near the entrance, his broad frame cutting through the illusion of effortless indulgence. He didn't belong here, and that was precisely why he was impossible to ignore. His sharp gaze sliced through the room, scanning faces, reading body language, absorbing every micro-expression.

When his eyes landed on her, Serena lifted her glass in an almost playful toast. He didn't return the gesture. Instead, he moved through the bar with quiet determination, his coat still damp from the streets below, his presence a stark contrast to the polished excess around him. No badge flashed, no gun drawn—he didn't need either. The weight of inevitability followed him, settling over Serena like a second skin.

"Interesting choice for a last drink," he said as he reached her table, his voice carrying over the ambient jazz and murmured deals being brokered in the background.

She smiled, slow and deliberate. "Is it my last?"

Stone didn't sit. He didn't offer pleasantries. He simply reached into his coat and placed something on the table between them. A single orchid, its delicate petals pristine under the dim glow of the bar's pendant lights. Lady Beatrice's orchid.

The air between them tightened. Serena's fingers grazed the stem, tracing its fragile edge.

"Poetic," she murmured. "But I imagine you have more than just flowers."

Stone's silence was answer enough. The noise of the bar seemed distant now, the rooftop's exclusivity providing an eerie cocoon. Serena leaned back, unfazed, legs crossed with practiced elegance.

"You always knew it would come to this, didn't you, Detective? You just didn't know where the story would end."

For the first time in a long time, Serena felt something close to admiration. Not for the law, not for the morality Stone believed in, but for him. For the way he had peeled back every layer, for the way he had hunted without ever losing himself to the game. But now, the game was over.

Stone finally broke the silence, his voice a low rumble that vibrated in the vast space.

"They called you the Angel of Justice," he said, the words laced with a bitter irony that mirrored my own internal turmoil. "But justice isn't about vengeance, is it? It's about balance, about restoring order. You created a chaos far greater than the one you sought to rectify."

His words struck a nerve, not because they were untrue, but because they were a stark, unvarnished reflection of the truth I was desperately trying to avoid. My justifications, my carefully constructed narratives, crumbled under the weight of his words, under the weight of the evidence he had meticulously gathered.

I had believed myself to be a righteous avenger, a corrector of societal imbalances. But the reality was far more brutal, far more disturbing. I was a destroyer, a wrecker of lives, a puppet of my own twisted desires.

He leaned forward, his eyes penetrating, unwavering.

"Tell me about the fear," he said, his voice barely a whisper. "Tell me about the terror of the victims. Tell me about the moments before the end. Paint me a picture, not of the elegant justice you sought, but of the raw, brutal reality of your actions."

He was asking me to confront the truth, not just the truth of my crimes, but the truth about myself. And it was a truth I had spent so long avoiding, burying beneath layers of carefully constructed lies and self-deception. It was a truth I had tried to suppress, to rewrite, to control.

I looked out at the city lights, a glittering expanse of beauty and decay, a reflection of the world I had tried to reshape with such bloody violence. I saw the faces of my victims, not just Alistair Finch, Arthur Blackwood, and Lady Beatrice, but the faces of those they left behind. The faces of their families, their colleagues, their friends, forever scarred by their absence. Their suffering felt like an immense weight on my soul.

The narrative shifted, not just in perspective, but in time. I found myself reliving the moments leading up to each killing. The thrill of the chase, the intoxicating power I felt as I manipulated my victims, playing with their fears, their hopes, their vulnerabilities.

I saw myself not as the righteous avenger, but as a predator, a manipulator, a skilled and ruthless killer. The trophies I had collected, once symbols of dark victory, now represented my descent into madness, the culmination of my obsessive desire for control.

The perspective shifted again, this time to the detective's viewpoint. We saw his obsession, his relentless pursuit, not just driven by the need to catch a killer, but by a gnawing suspicion that there was something deeper at play, something rotten at the heart of the society he served to protect.

Stone’s investigation delved into the dark underbelly of wealth and privilege, exposing the intricate web of deceit, corruption, and hypocrisy that thrived beneath the veneer of sophistication. He discovered the silent complicity of the wealthy elite, the intricate network of secrets and lies that enabled the injustices I had sought to redress.

His investigation wasn’t just about apprehending a killer; it was about uncovering the systemic failures that allowed such crimes to flourish. The more he discovered, the more he realized that my actions, while horrific, were a symptom of a deeper discomfort, a moral decay at the heart of a society that had become blind to its own failings.

The narrative then returns to my perspective, but a different me. A fractured me. A me who understands. The me that sees the complete lack of justice in my own twisted version of it. The me that had been a pawn all along. I, who had sought to punish the wicked, had become a monster myself, a reflection of the very flaws in the society that I had sought to destroy. The rain outside seemed to intensify, a relentless torrent mirroring the storm within my own psyche.

The final shift in perspective was the most chilling. It showed that my obsession was not with justice, but with control. I craved the power to manipulate, to dominate, to orchestrate the lives of others. My actions were not about righting wrongs, but about asserting my power over a world that felt chaotic and unpredictable. I had believed I was restoring order, but in reality, I had created a far greater disorder.

Perhaps justice wasn't served in any traditional sense. My apprehension would be a legal victory, but a psychological and societal reckoning would take much longer. My actions had shattered the illusion of perfection, revealing the flaws and the deep-seated corruption within the privileged class. The very act of my crimes, the public outcry, would change the world in unforeseen ways. The chaos I had created had exposed a festering wound at the heart of society, forcing it to confront its own moral failings.

Stone stood over the city, the distant hum of traffic below barely registering in his mind. The rooftop bar had emptied, leaving only the echoes of whispered conversations and the fading notes of jazz lingering in the night air. The weight of his choices pressed on him like an anchor, and for the first time in his career, he felt truly exposed.

"Tell me, Detective," Serena mused, swirling the last remnants of her drink, "Do you truly believe in justice? Or is it just another lie we tell ourselves to justify what we do?"

Stone exhaled sharply, his jaw tightening. He had spent years convincing himself that his actions were just, that the pursuit of criminals like her was noble, untainted by personal bias or vendetta. But now, as he stood before her, his moral compass wavered.

"Justice isn't a lie," he said finally, his voice low but steady. "But it's not as clean as people like to think. It's flawed, messy. It doesn't always mean what we want it to."

Serena leaned forward, intrigued. "And what do you want it to mean?" Her voice was almost tender, but Stone recognized it for what it was—an ultimate test.

His mind reeled with the memories of the case. The bodies, the cryptic clues, the grotesque beauty of Serena's meticulous planning. Serena chose every victim, and each death was a deliberate act of twisted retribution. She had played executioner, convinced she was evening the scales. But had she? Or had she merely indulged a hunger for control masked as justice?

Stone had his answer.

"Justice isn't revenge," he said, the words crystallizing into something undeniable. "And it isn't power. It's about balance, yes, but not in the way you see it. You didn't bring justice, Serena. You brought fear. Chaos. You replaced one kind of monster with another."

A slow smile tugged at Serena's lips, but there was no

victory in it.

"And yet, you hesitated before coming after me. Tell me, Stone—if I had killed the right people, would you have still hunted me? If I had only removed those truly deserving, by your code, would I still be here?"

Stone's silence stretched between them, thick and suffocating. Had he hesitated? Had there been a moment, deep in the recesses of his mind, where he had considered letting her go? He wanted to believe otherwise, but the doubt gnawed at him.

He shook his head. "It doesn't matter. The moment you decided you had the right to take lives, you became what you claimed to despise. I can't—won't—justify that."

Serena studied him for a long moment before she laughed, soft and almost sorrowful. "Then you've made your choice. I wondered if you would."

A beat of silence passed, then Stone pulled out his handcuffs. A silent command, impossible to ignore. "It's over."

Serena lifted her wrists, unresisting. As the metal closed around them, a strange sense of peace settled over her. "Perhaps it always was."

Stone exhaled sharply, the exhaustion of the chase weighing on him. "I knew it would end with you."

The wind shifted, carrying the sounds of the city upward —horns blaring, life moving on, oblivious to the quiet reckoning happening above.

Stone gestured toward the exit, and for a moment, Serena

simply stared at him, as if calculating whether there was still one final move to be made. Then, with a sigh—half amusement, half resignation—she stood, smoothing the silk of her dress.

"Shall we?" she said, her voice lilting, as if they were nothing more than old acquaintances departing from an evening of polite conversation.

Stone didn't answer. He only led her to the elevator, the city below unaware that, tonight, the rooftop bar had been the scene of something more than just another elite transaction.

As the doors slid shut, he felt something shift inside him—an unspoken resolution. Justice wasn't perfect. It never would be. But it was a choice, a commitment to something greater than personal vendetta. And tonight, he had chosen it.

38

The interrogation room felt colder now, the air thick with unspoken accusations. Stone’s gaze, usually sharp and unwavering, held a flicker of something akin to… pity? It was a fleeting expression, quickly masked again by his professional detachment, but it was enough to unsettle me.

Stone had pushed me to the edge, forcing me to confront the brutal reality of my actions, the chilling truth of my motives. And in that confrontation, something shifted within me. The carefully constructed veil, the righteous indignation, the meticulously crafted justifications—they all crumbled like sandcastles before a relentless tide.

He produced a small, tarnished silver locket. It wasn't one of my trophies, but it held a significance far greater than any diamond cufflink or sculpting knife. It was Evelyn’s locket. My sister’s locket. The one I’d worn as a child, a constant reminder of her innocent laughter and our shared dreams.

He said nothing, just laid it on the table between us, the tarnished silver catching the dim light. The silence was deafening, more oppressive than any interrogation tactic he’d used before.

The memories flooded back, a torrent of forgotten emotions, buried resentments, and simmering rage. It wasn't a sudden revelation, a dramatic epiphany, but a slow, agonizing dawning of a terrible truth. My crusade for ‘justice’, my elaborate game of cat and mouse with Stone. It had all been a distraction, a desperate attempt to mask a far deeper, far more personal wound.

Evelyn's death, ruled accidental, had never been accepted as such in my heart. The injustice, the unanswered questions, the simmering rage had festered, growing into a monstrous obsession that had consumed me entirely.

Each victim, each meticulously planned murder, had been a symbolic act of vengeance, a twisted ritualistic atonement for a loss I could never truly grieve. Arthur Blackwood, Alistair Finch, Baroness Anya Petrova, Lady Beatrice, Senator Harrison, Theo Graves—they were stand-ins, symbols of the privileged elite, their wealth and power representing the indifference that had allowed Evelyn's death to slip through the cracks, to be dismissed, to be forgotten.

I hadn't been seeking justice for society; I'd been seeking justice for myself, an impossible, bloody reckoning for a pain that could never be erased.

Stone, of course, hadn't seen that, not yet. He saw the pattern, but not the raw, agonizing grief at the heart of it all. He saw the killer, the predator, but not the broken sister, consumed by a grief so profound it had twisted her sanity. Stone thought he was closing in on a clever, manipulative sociopath. But he had no idea how close he was to the truth, a truth far more devastating, far more tragically human.

He spoke again, his voice barely above a whisper, "The last one... Isabelle."

My breath hitched. Isabelle. The name hung in the air, heavy with unspoken implications. Isabelle, my niece,

Evelyn's daughter, the one person I swore I would protect. The game, it seems, had taken a turn I hadn't anticipated. A turn that shattered the meticulously constructed narrative I had woven around my actions. I hadn't meant to hurt her.

The plan, however twisted, hadn't included her. But the chaos I had unleashed had caught her in its wake. A pawn in my twisted game of retribution, unintentionally sacrificed on the altar of my grief.

The irony was almost unbearable. I had sought to punish the perpetrators of injustice, and in doing so, I had become the ultimate perpetrator. My attempt to restore balance resulted in a far greater imbalance. I had attempted to heal a wound with bloodshed, leaving behind a chasm of pain far wider and deeper than the one I started with.

The narrative shifted once more, to a point in the past, to Isabelle's perspective. We see her as a young girl, filled with life, a vibrant personality with the same mischievous spark that Evelyn had once possessed. We see the impact my actions had on her, on her family, on her own delicate psyche. She'd witnessed the chaos I'd unleashed, not as an abstract concept, but as a personal tragedy. It wasn't just the death of her mother, but the shattering of her world.

The world in which a loving aunt transformed into a ruthless killer. The knowledge of my actions was a millstone, weighing down her childhood, poisoning her dreams, twisting her perception of the world and those she loved.

The shift back to my perspective was brutal. I saw myself not as a righteous avenger but as a destroyer, the architect of this devastating tragedy. I had created this chaos, and the pain that rippled through those close to me was my fault, my failure. I had sought to avenge my sister's death, to make those responsible pay, and in my twisted logic, I had succeeded. But the cost was too great, the victory hollow, the remorse unbearable.

Stone, in his own way, had won. Not by apprehending me, but by forcing me to confront the truth. The truth wasn't about elegant justice or the restoration of balance; it was about a broken woman, lost in the web of her own grief, blinded by her own pain. The game ended not with a dramatic arrest, but with a shattering realization.

My crusade for justice had destroyed everything I held dear. My hands, once tools of vengeful precision, were now stained not just with the blood of the rich and powerful, but with the blood of my own family. The game was over, and I was left with nothing but the ashes of my self-deception and the crushing weight of my guilt.

The rain outside finally ceased, leaving behind a strangely quiet cityscape. It was as if the city itself was holding its breath, waiting for the last act of this tragedy to unfold. But there was no last act. Just the quiet aftermath, the desolate landscape of a life destroyed by the very thing it sought to save.

Justice, in the end, was a cruel and elusive phantom, a twisted reflection of my self-destruction. The game had ended, but the consequence of my actions continued to reverberate, leaving an indelible scar on the world, and more importantly, on those I had purported to save. The true reckoning, it seemed, was only just beginning.

39

The memory of Evelyn's laughter, once a vibrant, joyful melody, now echoed in my ears as a mournful dirge. I remembered the day she died—the careless disregard, the missed opportunity for prevention, and how the wealthy elite dismissed her death as a tragic accident, a mere statistic, insignificant to their lives.

That was the injustice that simmered within me, that festered and mutated, slowly transforming me into a monster in my own eyes. I used each victim as a proxy, a stand-in for those who had allowed her death to be brushed aside, symbolically retaliating for a loss that would never be repaired.

I wasn't born evil. I didn't wake one morning with a thirst for blood or a desire for chaos. Once upon a time, I was cherished, loved, protected, and nurtured as a child, in a way. But the world, in its cold, indifferent brutality, had shattered the foundations of my existence. It took the light from my eyes and replaced it with a darkness I never knew existed.

My childhood home was a picturesque façade, a carefully crafted illusion that hid the simmering tensions beneath the surface. My parents, pillars of the community and the epitome of success and respectability, were consumed by a silent war, a battle fought with icy glares and unspoken resentments.

Their wealth, their status, the very things I had later come to revile, were the shackles that bound them, suffocating any genuine emotion or connection. They lived for appearances, for the accolades, for the validation of their peers, sacrificing everything—including their own children—on the altar of their ambition.

Evelyn and I found ourselves caught in the crossfire; our bond formed in the shared loneliness of a privileged but emotionally barren environment. She was the sunshine, I the shadow, perpetually seeking refuge in her warmth, her laughter the only antidote to the oppressive silence of our home.

Her death wasn't simply a tragedy; it was the final shattering of a fragile, illusory world. It was the revelation that the very people who were supposed to protect me were incapable of doing so, that the world I knew was a lie, a gilded cage concealing a brutal, indifferent truth.

This realization didn't blossom overnight. It was a gradual process, a creeping darkness that slowly consumed me. The initial shock and grief gave way to anger, a potent cocktail of rage and resentment that festered within me, poisoning my thoughts and shaping my actions.

The investigation into Evelyn's death was a farce, a perfunctory exercise designed to appease the concerned but ultimately indifferent authorities. The conclusion, an accidental death, was a cruel mockery of justice, a slap in the face to a grieving sister.

My destruction began long before my first act of violence. They sprouted in the stony soil of my childhood, nurtured by neglect and indifference, fueled by the simmering rage at the injustice of my sister's death and the complicity of a society that valued wealth and status above human life.

My warped sense of justice wasn't a sudden epiphany; it was a slow, agonizing metamorphosis, a transformation born from the ashes of my broken heart. It was a twisted, grotesque reflection of the system I sought to destroy, a perversion of the very principles of fairness and balance I claimed to champion.

But even in my madness, I wasn't entirely devoid of compassion. Isabelle, Evelyn's daughter, was the exception, the one constant flicker of light in my otherwise desolate existence. The thought of harming her was an abomination to me; yet she was caught in the whirlpool I'd created. A casualty of my twisted crusade, an innocent victim of my self-destructive obsession.

The last act of my 'justice', the culmination of my twisted game, had become a grotesque parody of itself. The carefully planned execution, the meticulous attention to detail, the symbolic nature of each act—all were meaningless now. They were mere footnotes in a tragedy of epic proportions, a self-inflicted wound that had left an indelible scar upon my soul and upon the lives of those I professed to love.

The rain outside had stopped, but a storm raged within. The interrogation room, with its cold, sterile environment, was a replica of the desolate landscape of my existence. There was no triumph, no satisfaction, no sense of closure. Only the crushing weight of my guilt, the unbearable burden of my actions.

The price of my twisted pursuit of justice was far greater than I could ever have imagined. The seeds of destruction, sown in the fertile ground of my grief, had yielded a bitter harvest indeed. And the bitter taste would remain a constant, searing reminder of the irreparable damage I had wrought.

The ultimate victim… that was the ultimate act of manipulation, the culmination of a long, horrifying game. It was a desperate attempt to exert ultimate control, a final, chilling statement. The victim's identity – that's something I won't reveal. You'll have to discover that for yourself. But know this: it was a betrayal, a profound and terrible act that further exposed the terrifying fragility of my mind, the complete dissolution of any semblance of morality or justice.

The broken mirrors, scattered across the landscape of my crimes, reflected not the flaws of society, but the shattered remnants of my soul. The illusion of justice shattered, leaving behind only the chilling reality of my depravity. And perhaps, that's the most terrifying realization of all: that the darkness I sought to vanquish in others lived, festering and growing, deep within myself.

The true crime wasn't the taking of lives; it was the methodical dismantling of my humanity, a slow, agonizing process I documented with each meticulously planned murder, each carefully selected trophy, each carefully crafted lie.

The silence in the aftermath, heavy with the weight of unconfessed sins, is a far more potent punishment than any sentence a judge could ever pronounce. The justice I sought was an illusion, a cruel and twisted mirage, ultimately leading only to my own destruction. And perhaps that's the only justice I deserve.

40

The weight of Serena's crimes did not rest solely on her shoulders; it seeped into Isabelle's life, an insidious poison that twisted her perception of love, trust, and justice. The child she had sworn to protect was now a casualty of her obsession, her innocence of collateral damage in a war she never chose to fight.

Isabelle had been young when Evelyn died, too young to fully grasp the complexities of loss but old enough to feel the emptiness it left behind. She had clung to Serena in the aftermath, seeking the warmth and protection that her mother's absence had stolen from her. But Serena, consumed by her thirst for vengeance, had been blind to the quiet fractures forming in Isabelle's world.

In the years that followed, Isabelle had grown into a quiet, introspective child, one who carried shadows in her eyes long before she understood their origin. She had learned early that grief was not something to be spoken of—it was a presence that lingered in the empty spaces, in the things left unsaid. Serena had been her guardian, but she had not been a source of comfort. Instead, she had become an enigma, a woman of contradictions: fiercely protective yet distant, loving yet consumed by something dark and unknowable.

At first, Isabelle had accepted it. She had learned to

navigate Serena's world, to tread lightly around the edges of her silences, to avoid the questions that seemed to unsettle her. But as she grew older, she noticed the inconsistencies, the way Serena's intensity would shift from warmth to something cold and impenetrable. There were nights when Serena would return home with eyes that burned too brightly, a strange, restless energy vibrating beneath her skin. There were moments when her words carried an edge, a quiet fury that hinted at something far more dangerous than mere grief.

Isabelle did not understand it then, but she felt it. And it frightened her.

She had idolized her aunt, had built her into something larger than life—a fierce protector, a woman who had survived unimaginable loss and had still stood strong. But when the truth unraveled, when the pieces of Serena's carefully concealed world began to fall apart, Isabelle's foundation cracked beneath her.

It had started with whispers. Questions asked in hushed tones, glances exchanged between strangers who thought she wasn't paying attention. And then, the news reports. The slow, dreadful realization that the woman she loved, the woman she trusted, was not who she claimed to be.

Serena had always spoken of justice, of righting the wrongs inflicted upon them, but the justice she pursued was not justice at all. It had been retribution, a vendetta that had spiraled so far out of control that it no longer resembled anything righteous. Isabelle had seen the names, the faces of the people Serena had deemed responsible, and she had felt sick.

Serena had painted them as villains, as cogs in a machine designed to protect the wealthy and the powerful, as people who had allowed Evelyn's death to be forgotten. But Isabelle had seen more than that. She had seen grieving families, people who had lost fathers, daughters, siblings. She had seen the ripples of Serena's actions stretching far beyond their intended targets, consuming innocent lives in the wake of her so-called justice.

And in that moment, Isabelle had realized the truth: Serena had become the very thing she claimed to despise.

The betrayal was not just in the crimes themselves, but in the deception—the years of half-truths and omissions, the careful construction of a world built on lies. Isabelle had spent her life believing in her aunt's strength, her unwavering sense of morality, only to discover that it had been nothing more than a carefully woven illusion.

She had been a pawn in Serena's crusade without ever knowing it. She had been raised in the shadow of a woman who had justified her own darkness under the guise of love and protection. And now, she was left to pick up the pieces of a life that had never truly belonged to her.

The weight of that realization crushed her.

No straightforward path forward existed, and no simple resolution to the war waged in her name was available. She could not erase the years of love and loyalty she had given to Serena, nor could she reconcile them with the horror of what her aunt had done. The memories of her childhood—the moments of warmth, the laughter, the whispered bedtime stories—were now tainted, colored by the knowledge that they had come from a woman capable of unimaginable cruelty.

In the days that followed Serena's arrest, Isabelle stood at a precipice, staring into the abyss that had claimed her aunt. She could allow the betrayal to consume her, to harden her heart the way it had hardened Serena's. She could let the bitterness take root, let the cycle of pain and vengeance continue.

Or she could choose something else.

She could walk away from the shadows that Serena had dragged her into. She could acknowledge the pain, the betrayal, the devastating loss of not just her mother but now the only other person she had truly loved—and she could refuse to let it define her.

Serena had believed she was acting for Isabelle, avenging Evelyn in a way the world had refused to. But she had never considered what Isabelle truly needed. Not revenge. Not blood. Not a war fought in her name.

She had needed love. Guidance. A family that did not view her as an extension of their grief, but as her own person. And now, for the first time in her life, she would have to build that for herself.

It would not be easy. The scars Serena had left on her soul would not fade overnight. But Isabelle would not become her aunt's legacy. She would not allow the darkness to consume her.

She would grieve. She would heal. And she would move forward—not as a victim, not as a pawn in someone else's war, but as the author of her own story.

For the first time, she would choose herself.

41

Detective Stone haunted me even in the silence of my cell. His face, etched with the weariness of a man who'd stared too long into the abyss, wouldn't leave my mind. He wasn't like the others, the ones who saw only a monster, a fiend. He saw the brokenness, the reflection of shattered lives in my eyes, and perhaps even a sliver of himself.

His own silence, a wall of impenetrable stoicism, mirrored my own carefully constructed façade. I wondered if he, too, carried the weight of unhealed wounds, the ghosts of past traumas whispering in the shadows of his soul.

He'd shown me photographs once, not of my victims, but of a decrepit farmhouse, half-buried in overgrown weeds. The paint was peeling, the windows broken, the air thick with the scent of decay and neglect. It was a picture of desolation, a visual representation of the childhood I'd described, a childhood steeped in a silent, pervasive violence that had never been acknowledged, never healed.

He didn't need to speak; the photograph spoke for itself. It was a mirror to my soul, a reflection of the broken home that had shaped me into the instrument of destruction I'd become. He saw the connection, the insidious link between my actions and the legacy of abuse. He saw the cycle, not just in my actions, but in the cyclical nature of trauma itself, the way it passed down through generations, leaving its scars on body and mind.

His own hands, I noticed during our interrogations, trembled slightly. Not a dramatic tremor, but a subtle, almost imperceptible twitch, a telltale sign of suppressed anxiety. It spoke of a history he hadn’t shared, a burden he carried silently. There was a quiet intensity in his gaze, a profound sadness that went beyond the professional detachment of a seasoned detective.

I glimpsed a reflection of my own haunted eyes in his, a shared understanding of the lingering wounds that refuse to heal. The victims, they were more than just statistics, more than just names on a list. They were reflections of my pain, the mirrors through which I saw my own fractured reflection, my self-destruction. And Stone, in his own way, saw the same reflection in my eyes, a deeper understanding of the enduring impact of trauma.

The physical wounds were easier to address, easier to quantify. The scars on my arms, the result of my mother's rage, were visible reminders of a past I couldn't escape. Each mark, a testament to the violence that had shaped my life, a roadmap to the fractured psyche I had become. But the mental scars, the psychological wounds, those were far more insidious, far more pervasive.

They ran deeper than skin, seeping into my very being, shaping my perceptions, influencing my actions, controlling my every move. The fear, the constant, gnawing anxiety, the feeling of being perpetually on edge—these were invisible wounds, invisible chains that bound me to the past, ensuring my descent into darkness.

Stone, he understood the invisible wounds, too. The way he watched me, the subtle shifts in his demeanor, the lingering silences, all spoke of a shared understanding, a mutual recognition of the deep, lasting impact of trauma. He knew my actions weren't merely random acts of savagery; they were the result of a lifetime of unhealed wounds, a desperate attempt to exert control over a life that had always felt chaotic and out of control.

His patience, his persistent refusal to judge, it was a tacit acknowledgment of the cyclical nature of trauma, the way it passed from generation to generation, leaving its indelible mark on lives forever changed.

The cycle, I knew, wouldn't end with me. Generations to come would be touched by the ripple effects of the violence and trauma I had inflicted and caused. The legacy of unhealed wounds, the inheritance of pain and suffering—these were far more potent than any physical weapon, any physical act of violence.

Stone, in his silent way, acknowledged this. He understood the profound weight of inherited trauma, the cyclical nature of violence, the way it perpetuates itself across time, leaving a trail of destruction in its wake. The unspoken understanding, the shared weight of knowledge, made our encounters different from the usual cat-and-mouse game between killer and detective. It was a dance between two broken souls.

His silence, his quiet observation, became a form of empathy. It wasn't sympathy, not pity; it was a deep, unsettling understanding of the dark forces that had shaped us both. The broken mirrors we saw in each other's eyes reflected not just the pain we had inflicted, but the pain we had endured, the suffering we had inherited, the wounds that refuse to heal.

The silence between us, far from being empty, resonated

with the unspoken echoes of shattered lives, broken homes, generational violence, and our shared, inescapable destiny. The silence was a testament to the enduring power of trauma, to the way it shapes our lives, dictates our choices, and condemns us to repeat the mistakes of the past.

The echoes of that farmhouse, that symbol of neglect and abuse, continued to resonate within me, even in the sterile confines of my prison cell. Stone's gaze, his silent acknowledgment, was a recognition of that legacy, a shared understanding of the darkness that binds us, a shared burden of inherited wounds that run deeper than skin, a testament to the unrelenting force of cyclical violence that refuses to be broken.

It's in the silence, the absence of straightforward answers, that the true horror lies. The cycle is not a story; it's a sentence, a life sentence served in the prison of our own making. The truth of our shared experience, the weight of unhealed wounds, is too heavy for words to ever fully convey.

It is a heavy, chilling, unforgiving silence that follows the storm of violence. It's in that silence that both the killer and the detective find themselves forever bound by the relentless power of a cycle that knows no end.

42

The cold steel of the cell door, a constant, metallic presence, felt less like a barrier and more like a reflection of my internal landscape—rigid, unforgiving, and utterly desolate. Stone’s visits had ceased, his silent understanding replaced by the monotonous routine of prison life.

The silence, once filled with unspoken truths, had become a suffocating emptiness, a void echoing the hollowness within me. Yet, even within this bleak confinement, a seed of something else had taken root—a faint, flickering ember of something that might, perhaps, be called hope.

It wasn’t a sudden epiphany, a dramatic shift in perspective. It was more subtle, a gradual dawning awareness that the cycle of violence didn't have to continue. That my actions, while horrific and unforgivable, weren’t an immutable destiny. I dissected my own pathology with a newfound objectivity, peeling back the layers of trauma and manipulation that had shaped my warped worldview.

I started with the smallest things. I joined a prison book club, a ridiculously mundane activity, yet it was a first step outside the suffocating walls of my self-imposed isolation. The discussions, initially awkward and stilted, gradually opened a space for genuine connection, however fragile. The shared experience of literature, the exploration of human emotions, both dark and light, allowed me to see the world beyond the confines of my pain.

The women in the book club, each with their own stories of struggle and survival, were unexpected mirrors. They weren't reflections of my darkness, but rather refractions, showing the possibilities of resilience, of finding strength in shared vulnerability. Their lives were as scarred as mine, yet they showed a capacity for empathy, for forgiveness, for the quiet, persistent act of rebuilding.

One woman, a former drug addict named Maria, shared her story with a heartbreaking honesty. She paved her path with violence and despair, yet found a path towards redemption, escaping the cycle of addiction and self-destruction.

Her words were a revelation, a living testament to the possibility of change, even in the face of seemingly insurmountable obstacles. Listening to her, I saw a reflection of myself, not in the darkness of my past, but in the potential for healing, for transformation.

My own attempts at self-reflection were fraught with difficulties. The fragmented memories, the buried emotions, resisted surfacing. The therapy sessions were agonizing, a painful excavation of a past I had tried so hard to bury.

The therapist, a woman with a calm, unwavering gaze, didn't judge my actions. She didn't offer simple answers or facile reassurances. Instead, she provided a safe space for exploration, a framework for understanding the roots of my violence, without condoning it.

The process was excruciatingly slow, each breakthrough punctuated by setbacks, by waves of self-loathing and despair. But the very act of facing my past, of acknowledging the depth of my culpability, was a crucial step towards healing.

The rationalizations, the carefully constructed narratives I had used to justify my actions, crumbled under the weight of the truth. The monstrous persona I had cultivated, the carefully crafted image of a cold, calculating killer, was merely a mask, a defense mechanism built to shield a vulnerable, wounded child.

I started writing again, not as a means of self-justification, but as catharsis. The words flowed differently this time, not as a celebration of violence, but as an exploration of pain, of regret, of the desperate longing for redemption. The stories were not about the victims, but about the unseen wounds, the silent screams, the unspoken trauma that had shaped my life.

The writing became a form of therapy, a way to confront my demons, to acknowledge the immense suffering I had caused, and to begin the long, arduous journey towards healing. It was a way to make amends, not to the victims, for that was impossible, but to myself, to the fractured fragments of my soul. Each word written was a step further away from the abyss, a step closer to a fragile, uncertain future.

The path to redemption was not a linear one, free from setbacks and regressions. There were moments of doubt, of overwhelming despair, when the weight of my past threatened to consume me once more. But the support of the book club, the unwavering presence of my therapist, and the quiet, persistent act of writing, these were anchors in the storm, preventing me from being swept away by the tide of self-hatred.

The possibility of forgiveness remained elusive. The victims' families would never forgive me, and rightly so. My hope for redemption wasn't about erasing the past or seeking absolution; it was about transforming the destructive forces within me, about breaking the cycle of violence that had defined my life. It was about using my experience, my knowledge, my pain, to help others avoid the same tragic path. It was about offering something of value in return for the immeasurable harm I had caused.

The echoes of the farmhouse, the symbol of my broken childhood, still resonated within me. But now, a new sound joined the echoes: the quiet whisper of hope, a faint promise of a future where I might finally break the cycle of violence. The mirror, once reflecting only a distorted image of destruction, now showed a flicker of something different—a fragile reflection of resilience, of the persistent human capacity for change, for growth, for redemption.

The journey was far from over; the scars remained indelible reminders of a past I could never erase. But the journey itself, the slow, painful process of confronting the darkness within and striving towards the light, was the beginning of my redemption.

The silence, once filled with the heavy weight of unhealed wounds, now held the faint, almost imperceptible sound of hope, a quiet testament to the enduring power of the human spirit. The silence, finally, became a space not of condemnation, but of possibility.

43

The art of manipulation, I learned, wasn’t about brute force or overt coercion. It was far more subtle, a delicate dance of suggestion and persuasion, a carefully orchestrated symphony of psychological cues designed to elicit the desired response. It was about understanding the vulnerabilities of others, their unspoken desires, their deepest fears—and then using that knowledge to bend them to my will.

My victims weren't simply targets; they were intricate puzzles, each with their own unique set of weaknesses. I studied them meticulously, observing their routines, listening to their conversations, absorbing every detail that revealed their insecurities, their hidden desires, their carefully constructed facades.

It started with observation, a patient accumulation of data. Their social media profiles were goldmines of information, revealing their aspirations, their anxieties, their intimate relationships. A casual glance at their wardrobe choices spoke volumes about their self-perception, their attempts to project a specific image to the world.

The way they held themselves, their mannerisms, their vocal patterns—all of these seemingly insignificant details contributed to a larger picture, a detailed psychological profile that allowed me to anticipate their reactions, to predict their responses.

Mirroring was a potent tool. Subtly mimicking their body language, their speech patterns, their even their emotional tones, created a sense of rapport, a feeling of connection and understanding. It was a subconscious form of flattery, a way of establishing trust and breaking down their defenses. Once they were comfortable, once their guard was down, the manipulation could begin in earnest.

Then came the strategic deployment of carefully chosen words. Language is a powerful weapon, capable of shaping perceptions, influencing emotions, and manipulating thoughts. I mastered the art of suggestion, planting seeds of doubt, subtly shifting their perspectives, guiding their decisions without them even realizing they were being manipulated. The power of suggestion lay in its insidious nature; the idea, once planted, took root in their minds, nurtured by their own insecurities and biases.

Framing was another essential technique. By handpicking the words and phrases I used, I could subtly alter the context, shaping their perception of events, influencing their interpretations of reality. A simple change of wording, a carefully placed adjective, could completely transform the narrative, making the undesirable seem desirable, the absurd seem plausible, the impossible seem inevitable.

Using emotional appeals was crucial. By tapping into their hopes, their fears, their sense of self-worth, I could elicit the desired emotional responses, making them more susceptible to influence. Fear was a potent motivator, making them compliant, making them hesitant to question or resist. Sympathy was another effective tactic, creating a sense of obligation, making them feel responsible for my well-being, making them more willing to accommodate my needs.

People also underestimated the power of silence.

Sometimes, we achieved the most effective manipulation through inaction—strategically omitting information and using carefully crafted silences to let the imagination fill in the gaps, creating mystery, anticipation, and suspense. This subtle pressure, this implied threat, was often far more effective than any explicit threat or demand.

Gaslighting was another insidious tactic. Subtly distorting their perception of reality, making them question their own sanity, their own memories, their own judgment. It was a way of undermining their confidence, eroding their sense of self, making them more dependent on my interpretation of events.

And finally, there was the manipulation of their social environment. By subtly influencing their relationships with others, I could isolate them, making them more vulnerable and dependent on me. By creating discord among their friends and family, I could erode their support network, making them more susceptible to my influence.

It was a complex and multifaceted process, a symphony of psychological techniques carefully orchestrated to achieve my goals. The victims were not merely passive recipients of my manipulations; they were active participants, their own vulnerabilities and insecurities playing a crucial role in their susceptibility. The process was, in a perverse way, a collaboration—a dance between predator and prey, a deadly ballet of deception and desire.

The satisfaction wasn't just in the act itself, but in the exquisite control, the almost artistic precision with which I orchestrated their downfall. It was a performance, and I was the master puppeteer, pulling the strings, directing the show, enjoying the subtle, almost imperceptible shifts in their expressions as their carefully constructed worlds crumbled around them.

Their helplessness, their utter dependence—that was the ultimate reward. Their destruction's exquisite, chilling symphony was a masterpiece, showcasing the human mind's power of creation and destruction. The beauty, the elegance, the sheer artistry of manipulation—that was the allure, the intoxicating pull that kept me coming back for more. The thrill was not just in the taking of a life, but in the slow, meticulous dismantling of a person's reality, the systematic erosion of their self-worth, their independence, their very being.

The trophies I took were not just symbolic representations of power; they were concrete reminders of my mastery, tangible evidence of my complete and utter control. Each object held a memory, a whisper of a life extinguished, a testament to my manipulative prowess. They were not mere souvenirs; they were trophies, symbols of conquest, artifacts of my chilling art.

Each one, a perfect, chillingly beautiful testament to my skill. They were more than trophies; they were extensions of myself, pieces of the puzzle that formed my perverse, twisted identity. They tangibly proved my ability to manipulate, control, and dominate. These fruits were a reward for my meticulous planning, artistic skill, and hard work.

44

The truth, as they say, is subjective. Or perhaps more accurately, it's malleable, a putty in the hands of a skilled sculptor. I, of course, am a master sculptor of truth, shaping and molding it to fit my narrative, to justify my actions.

My reality isn't a reflection of objective facts; it's a carefully constructed monument, built upon layers of self-deception, rationalization, and carefully chosen omissions. Each brick is a carefully placed lie, a half-truth, a distorted perspective, all meticulously arranged to support the grand facade of my self-justification.

Consider the victims. They weren't simply victims; they were symbols, embodiments of a corrupt system. Their wealth, their privilege, their callous indifference to the suffering of others—these were the justifications, the rationalizations that fueled my actions. I didn't murder them; I corrected them. I removed the cancer from the body politic, restoring a balance that had been cruelly disrupted by generations of inequality and injustice.

This wasn't a spontaneous eruption of violence; it was a meticulously planned operation, a surgical strike against the heart of societal rot. With chilling efficiency, they selected each target with surgical precision, dissecting and analyzing their lives to exploit their vulnerabilities. Their opulent lifestyles, their casual cruelty, their sense of entitlement—these were not random characteristics; they were precisely the traits that marked them as deserving of my 'corrective justice'.

My manipulation went beyond the victims themselves. I crafted a narrative, a story that would resonate with those who felt marginalized, ignored, disenfranchised by the very system that those victims represented.

I used the media, the internet, the whispers of fear and uncertainty to shape public opinion, to sow seeds of doubt and distrust. My actions were not random acts of violence, but part of a larger plan, a carefully orchestrated campaign designed to expose the corruption and hypocrisy of the elite.

The detective, obsessed with catching me, was merely another pawn in my game. His relentless pursuit, his obsession with solving the puzzle, only amplified my narrative, to draw more attention to the flaws of the system, to the systemic injustices that made my actions, in my mind, not only justifiable but necessary. His frustration, his inability to grasp the true nature of my actions, only strengthened my resolve, to reinforce my belief in the righteousness of my cause.

The construction of this reality required considerable skill, an understanding of psychology, of human behavior, of the power of suggestion and manipulation. It's about understanding the vulnerabilities, the weaknesses, the insecurities of others—and using that knowledge to craft a narrative that resonates with their pre-existing biases and beliefs.

It involved the careful selection and presentation of facts, the strategic omission of crucial details, the framing of events in a manner that supports the desired interpretation. It's about controlling the narrative, shaping the perception of reality, ensuring that my actions are viewed not as acts of violence, but as acts of justice, or perhaps even as acts of art.

I paint a picture, a carefully constructed reality, in which I am not a murderer but a revolutionary, not a criminal but a savior, not a monster but a misunderstood heroine. I play with the boundaries of perception, blurring the lines between right and wrong, creating ambiguity where there should be clarity, and doubt where there should be certainty.

The process is not merely a manipulation of facts, but a manipulation of emotions. I exploit the inherent human desire for justice, for retribution, for revenge. I appeal to the sense of outrage at inequality, at the hypocrisy of the wealthy and powerful. I feed off their anger, frustration, and resentment to fuel my narrative.

I do it with such subtle artistry, such chilling precision, that those who observe my actions—the ones who are captivated by the drama—become active participants in my own twisted reality. They become complicit, not in my actions themselves, but in the acceptance of my narrative, in the validation of my warped sense of justice. They don't just witness my crimes; they become co-conspirators, silently endorsing my actions through their continued fascination, their inability to turn away from the chilling spectacle of my carefully constructed reality.

The final victim, my masterpiece, is a testament to this manipulative power. Their identity is carefully chosen, a symbol of the very system I seek to dismantle. Their death is not an end, but a culmination, a final, powerful statement that will resonate for years to come, a chilling reminder of the consequences of unchecked power and systemic corruption.

The aftermath of the crime isn't chaos; it's a new order, a world reordered according to my twisted vision of justice. The silence after the storm isn't just silence; it's the quiet acceptance of my carefully constructed reality, the subtle shift in the perception of what is right, what is wrong, what is just, and what is not.

And the reader? You are inextricably bound to this narrative, a participant in this twisted game of perception, this dance between reality and illusion. Your reaction, your complicity, your ultimate judgment of my actions… that is the accurate measure of my success, the final, chilling validation of the power of a carefully constructed reality.

45

The insidious nature of lies, I've come to realize, isn't simply about the falsehood itself. It's the slow, corrosive effect they have on everything they touch. It's a poison that seeps into the very fabric of relationships, twisting trust into suspicion, certainty into doubt.

My own life is a testament to this, a tapestry woven with threads of deceit, where the truth is a frayed, almost invisible, element. Each lie, no matter how insignificant it initially seemed, chipped away at the foundations of my reality, until the edifice crumbled, leaving behind only the hollow shell of what once was.

Take, for instance, my relationship with my mother. It was a complex, volatile entanglement built on a foundation of carefully constructed illusions. She had always presented a facade of effortless grace, a picture of upper-class sophistication and effortless charm.

Beneath that polished exterior, however, was a woman consumed by insecurities and a desperate need for control. Her lies weren't grand pronouncements, but rather a series of carefully curated omissions, subtle distortions of reality designed to maintain her carefully crafted image.

She lied about her past, omitting details that didn't fit the narrative she wished to project. Concealing debts and financial struggles, she deceptively portrayed an image of opulent extravagance. She lied about her relationships, masking the emptiness beneath her social success with fabricated tales of romance and companionship. These lies, individually insignificant, collectively created a suffocating atmosphere of deceit, poisoning our relationship from the inside out.

It wasn't just her lies; my own contributions to this tapestry of deception were equally significant. Early on, I realized the fastest way to win her approval was by following her lead and repeating her meticulously constructed stories. I adopted her methods, mastering the art of subtle omission, of crafting my own realities to fit her expectations. I became a master of deception, mirroring her own manipulative tactics, and in doing so, I lost a part of myself.

The corrosive effect of these lies extended far beyond our immediate relationship. It permeated my worldview, shaping my perceptions and influencing my choices. I saw the world through a lens of deception, where appearances mattered more than substance, and where truth was a malleable commodity to be shaped and molded to fit one's needs.

This realization, the understanding of how deeply lies had poisoned my life, was a crucial turning point. It was the beginning of my descent into the darkness, a dark path where I sought to balance the perceived injustices of the world through my own acts of twisted justice.

Each murder was, in a warped sense, corrective action, an attempt to redress the imbalances I perceived in society. But each act of violence was also a lie, a deception, both to myself and the world. I justified my actions, constructed elaborate rationalizations, creating a narrative that painted me as a righteous avenger. This self-deception was a crucial component of my actions, allowing me to suppress the guilt and remorse that should have consumed me.

Detective Stone was a master of deception in his own right. His methods were more subtle than mine, more insidious. He didn't use blatant lies; instead, he used the power of omission, of carefully crafted silences, and strategic leaks to the media. He created a narrative, shaping public opinion and influencing the course of the investigation. He selectively released information to the press, designed to guide public perception and manipulate fear and anxiety.

He manipulated not only public opinion but also the emotions of the victims' families. He expressed empathy and understanding, skillfully extracting information while fostering trust. This was a calculated deception, a masterful manipulation of human emotions designed to achieve his objectives.

Stone's ability to control the flow of information and manipulate emotional responses was a testament to his own skill in deception. He used the media's insatiable appetite for detail to his advantage, crafting a narrative that subtly implicated me while maintaining a facade of tireless pursuit.

His lies were not crude pronouncements of falsehood, but rather the strategic manipulation of truth, the subtle distortion of reality, the carefully orchestrated omission of crucial details. This was a different corrosion, a slow poisoning of the investigation, designed to lead me into his meticulously laid trap.

The media, too, played a significant role in this grand deception. The insatiable public hunger for sensational details, the relentless pursuit of information, the constant speculation and conjecture, all contributed to the construction of a distorted reality. Because of Stone's strategic leaks and carefully crafted statements, the media's portrayal of events heightened the sense of chaos and uncertainty, confusing truth and fiction.

The corrosive power of lies extends beyond individual relationships and criminal investigations. It touches every aspect of society, shaping our perceptions, influencing our decisions, and distorting our understanding of reality.

Political rhetoric, advertising campaigns, and even casual conversations are rife with subtle deceptions, half-truths, and carefully crafted omissions. These lies, individually insignificant, collectively contribute to a climate of distrust and uncertainty.

The ability to discern truth from falsehood is a crucial skill in navigating the complexities of modern life. The consequences of succumbing to deception can be devastating, leading to fractured relationships, misguided actions, and a profound sense of disillusionment.

My story serves as a stark reminder of the corrosive power of lies, a cautionary tale about the dangers of self-deception and the devastating consequences of manipulating reality. The ultimate tragedy is not simply the acts themselves, but the erosion of truth and trust that lies at their heart. It's a slow, insidious decay that leaves behind only ruins and shattered fragments of what once was—a truth reflected in the shattered pieces of my existence.

The game isn't about winning or losing; it's about the relentless, corrosive power of lies, a power that leaves its mark on everything it touches. And I, in my own twisted way, was a testament to that power.

46

The city, draped in the opulent silks of its own self-importance, was a breeding ground for the kind of violence I craved. It wasn't the grit and grime of the alleyways that fueled my actions; it was the polished surfaces, the gleaming facades, the insidious hypocrisy that lurked beneath the veneer of civility. It was the blatant disregard for the suffering of others, the casual cruelty masked by smiles and charitable donations, that ignited the fire within me. They lived in gilded cages, oblivious to the suffering just beyond their meticulously manicured lawns. Their lives were a performance, a carefully orchestrated illusion designed to mask the emptiness at their core.

I saw it in the hollow eyes of the debutantes, their smiles as brittle as the champagne flutes they clinked. I saw it in the cold ambition of the CEOs, their ruthlessness masked by tailored suits and carefully crafted public images. I saw it in the detached indifference of the politicians, their promises as empty as the promises they made to those who truly needed them. These were the people who built their empires on the backs of the forgotten, the overlooked, the discarded. They were the architects of a system designed to benefit only the privileged few, leaving the rest to fend for themselves in a world of escalating inequality.

The system itself, I believed, was complicit. Those with

the means and the influence easily circumvented the laws that were designed to protect. The wealthy and powerful escaped accountability by frequently manipulating the justice system, despite its reputation for impartiality.

The police, meant to uphold the law, were often more concerned with maintaining order than with achieving justice, turning a blind eye to the suffering of the marginalized. It was a tapestry woven with threads of injustice, a web of interconnected failures that left the vulnerable exposed to exploitation and abuse.

Their wealth, their power, their influence—these were shields against accountability, allowing them to perpetuate a system that benefited them at the expense of others. They saw themselves as superior, as entitled to their privileged positions, oblivious to the suffering they inflicted on those less fortunate.

Their blindness to the consequences of their actions was a sickness, a moral decay that ran deeper than any single individual. It wasn't just about their individual failings; it was about the systemic failures that allowed their cruelty to flourish.

Each of my victims represented a different facet of this systemic failure, a different manifestation of the moral decay I sought to eradicate. They were the architects of a world built on inequality, a world where the privileged few thrived at the expense of the many. My actions were, in my warped worldview, a form of social commentary, a radical response to a system that had failed to protect its most vulnerable members. I was a mirror reflecting the dark side of their carefully constructed reality, a dark reflection of the rot at the heart of their privileged world.

But the truth is more nuanced than the narrative I

constructed for myself. The rationalizations, the justifications, the elaborate self-deceptions—they were all part of the tapestry of lies I wove around myself to mask the guilt, the remorse, the terrifying emptiness at my core.

The societal failings I observed were undeniable, but they did not justify my actions. They did not excuse the violence, the pain, the suffering I inflicted. My actions were not acts of social justice; they were acts of unadulterated violence, driven by a twisted sense of morality and a deep-seated need for control.

Stone understood this better than I did. He saw through my carefully crafted narrative, recognizing the darkness that fueled my actions. He didn't focus on the societal issues I used as justification; instead, he focused on me, on the darkness that resided within.

Stone saw the flaws in my logic, the inconsistencies in my narrative, the cracks in the façade I presented to the world. He understood that while societal structures may contribute to the environment in which violence can flourish; they don't determine the individual choices we make. He understood that the ultimate responsibility rests with the individual.

And perhaps that's the most unsettling truth of all. The societal roots of violence are complex, extending far beyond individual acts. But the choice to act violently, to inflict pain and suffering, ultimately rests with the individual. The system may fail, but we are still responsible for our actions, for the choices we make within the confines of that failing system.

My own actions are a stark reminder of that ultimate truth, a testament to the darkness that can live within even the most carefully constructed facade. My story, a twisted reflection of a broken system, is ultimately a story of individual culpability. The question remains: who is truly responsible—the system, or the individual who chooses to exploit it? The answer, I fear, is both. And that is the true horror.

47

Stone had always prided himself on the line he walked—between justice and revenge, between right and wrong. It had never been easy, but he had made it work. The law had been his guide, his constant, his tool. It was what allowed him to stay sane when everything else seemed like chaos. But as the investigation progressed, as the pieces of the puzzle fell into place and he faced the killer more directly, that line became harder to see.

My actions weren't random. Each victim was a calculated target, carefully selected from among the wealthy, the powerful, those who had used their position to trample over the less fortunate. My logic was simple, and in some ways, it was compelling. He had acted where the system had failed, where justice had been elusive for too long. There was something raw and honest in his fury, something that spoke to Stone's own frustrations. How many times had Stone sat in courtrooms, watching the rich and untouchable twist the law to their advantage, all while the victims—the ones who mattered most—remained nameless, forgotten, or worse, silenced?

Stone's first instinct had been to stop the killers, to bring them to justice. That had always been his mission—to uphold the law, to protect the vulnerable from those who thought they were above the rules. But as this particular case wore on, he began to question whether justice, as he had always known it, was really what he was chasing anymore.

The more he watched my methods—how I targeted those who manipulated the system for their own gain, how I exposed the fragility of the law with every kill—the more Stone saw himself in him. Not in the violence or the bloodshed, but in the anger that fueled each act, in the disillusionment with a system that had failed too many times to count.

Stone had spent years, decades even, enforcing laws that often seemed out of reach for those who needed them most. He had spent countless nights wondering why the powerful always seemed to get away with their sins, while the powerless suffered. He realized I was right in one regard. The system wasn't just flawed, it was broken. And while Stone had tried to fix it from within, to right its wrongs through investigations, arrests, and paperwork, the more he saw my work, the more he questioned whether any of it mattered. What was the point of following a broken system when it couldn't deliver the justice it promised? What was the point of playing by the rules when the rules were rigged in favor of the very people who deserved punishment?

And that was where the ambiguity began. It wasn't a clean line between right and wrong anymore. If justice was only achievable for a select few, if the system protected the guilty while punishing the innocent, then what did that make him? What did that make the killers? Were they both just pawns in the same game, caught between ideals that were as unattainable as they were necessary?

Stone had tried to separate himself from my motivations, to draw a clear boundary between his own sense of duty and my twisted sense of retribution. But every time he thought he had me figured out, every time he believed he could compartmentalize his role as the cop and my role as the criminal, something would shake him.

My message has always been clear: The system is broken. The law is flawed. And if justice cannot be served, then it is up to me to deliver it. It was a sentiment Stone had heard in his own thoughts many times. The more he followed the trail, the more he found himself wondering: was this really justice? Or was this just another form of vengeance?

I believed I was doing what the system could not. But Stone knew better. He knew that vengeance, no matter how justified it seemed, could never be a replacement for justice. He had seen the consequences of personal vendettas time and time again—how they consumed people, turned them into something monstrous. My actions, as much as they might have seemed like a righteous crusade, were only feeding into the same cycle of violence that had long plagued the city.

But then, Stone had to ask himself: was she any different? Her motivations had never been as clear-cut as he had once believed. Yes, she had a deep sense of duty, a belief in the law. But she also had a deep, unspoken rage—rage at a system that didn't seem to care about the people it was meant to protect. Rage at the wealthy and powerful who could bend the law to their will, and the broken bodies left behind in their wake.

Stone had told himself for years that he was chasing justice, that he was fighting for the victims who could not fight for themselves. But deep down, he couldn't shake the feeling that it wasn't just justice he was after—it was something more personal. It was the satisfaction of bringing down those who had wronged the system, the rush of seeing them finally held accountable. He had allowed his anger to cloud his judgment, just like I had done.

The difference between him and I was that Stone still believed in the possibility of a solution, that there was a way to bring people to justice within the system. But as the weeks wore on, the cracks in that belief were becoming harder to ignore. How many times had the system let him down? How many times had he watched the powerful walk free while the powerless paid the price?

It wasn't until we came together at the rooftop bar that Stone faced the full weight of this moral conflict. The final moment, Stone had to decide whether to pull the trigger to end it all for the sake of justice, or to hold back, to take me in and allow the law to have its due course. It felt like a test he couldn't pass. My words echoed in his mind: The system is broken. It's time for someone to fix it.

But Stone couldn't fix it, not on his own. And if he gave in to the temptation to take matters into his own hands, what did that make him? What would it say about the very principles he had fought for all his life?

Stone didn't pull the trigger, obviously. He didn't even take his firearm out. He didn't need to. His decision wasn't based on some grand, altruistic belief in the law. It was simply this: I am not her. I had chosen the path of violence, of vengeance, and Stone refused to follow. Even if the system was broken, even if it was deeply flawed, they still only had that system. The moment he crossed that line—if he crossed that line—he would be no better than me.

In that instant, Stone realized that justice was not about the ideal of a perfect system. It was about the work, the daily struggle to hold on to what was right, despite the flaws, despite the failures. Justice was about the fight, not the victory. And as he handcuffed me and took me away that evening, Stone felt a small sense of peace—a decision made, a line drawn, even if it wasn't as clear as he would have liked.

48

The courtroom exuded a sense of history and grandeur, with high ceilings and intricate wooden beams. Soft golden light streamed through tall, arched windows, casting a warm glow over polished oak furniture. The judge's mahogany bench stood at the front, beneath a grand coat of arms, symbolizing authority. Plush velvet seats lined the room, contrasting with gleaming brass accents. The scent of aged wood and leather-bound books filled the air, as the quiet anticipation of justice hung over the space where truth and decision awaited.

Detective Stone sat in the front row, his face impassive, his eyes betraying nothing. He'd become a fixture in my life, a shadow, a constant reminder of the inescapable consequences of my actions. But even his unwavering gaze couldn't penetrate the carefully constructed façade I'd erected, the carefully curated narrative I'd presented to the world.

The prosecution, fueled by righteous indignation and a desperate need to paint me as a monster, presented a distorted image of my motivations, reducing them to simple acts of sadistic violence. They failed to grasp the deeper complexities, the nuanced layers of my actions. They failed to see the invisible wounds.

They showcased the physical evidence: the meticulously

chosen trophies, each a testament to my meticulous planning and my profound understanding of human psychology. They paraded witnesses who described the terror, the devastation, the irreversible damage inflicted upon the victims and their families.

They painted a picture of pure evil, of a calculating predator who stalked the city's elite, leaving a trail of death and destruction in her wake. They were right, of course, in the broadest strokes. But they missed the subtle nuances, the underlying currents of societal decay that fueled my actions.

The defense, predictably, tried to portray me as a victim myself, a woman driven mad by societal injustices, a pawn in a larger game of systemic oppression. They pointed to the inequalities rampant in the city, the vast abyss between the wealthy elite and the impoverished masses, the casual cruelty that permeated the very fabric of society. They argued my actions were a desperate, albeit twisted, attempt to achieve justice in a system that had utterly failed.

The judge, a weary man with eyes that had seen too much, seemed to understand, at least in some small part, the complexities of the situation. He recognized the systemic failures that allowed such disparities to exist; the invisible wounds that ran deeper than any physical wound, infecting society like a malignant disease.

However, the legal system, in its rigid structure and adherence to outdated procedures, was ill-equipped to address such nuanced issues. In that sterile courtroom, the dispensing of justice was a blunt instrument, incapable of addressing the insidious damage inflicted by a society that prioritized profit over people.

The system failed the victims, their families, and even me. It failed to address the root causes of crime, the systemic injustices that bred a climate of despair and violence. It was designed to allocate punishment. But it couldn't offer redress; it couldn't heal the wounds; it couldn't bring back the dead. It only offered a superficial sense of closure, a hollow satisfaction that failed to address the underlying issues that festered beneath the surface of society.

The media frenzy surrounding the trial further amplified the sense of injustice. The headlines shrieked about the 'Angel of Death', the 'Nightingale of Despair', reducing my actions to sensationalist narratives devoid of context. They showed photos of me, my face perpetually impassive, as if any expression would betray the intricate layers of my motivations, the carefully constructed edifice of my personality.

The public clamored for retribution, for punishment, demanding that the system swiftly deliver a sense of closure. But closure, true closure, would never be found in a courtroom, in a judge's gavel, or in a prison sentence.

My actions were a symptom of a larger illness, a reflection of society's failure to address the fundamental inequalities that bred such despair. The system punished the symptom, not the disease. It focused on the individual act of violence, ignoring the systemic failures that created the environment in which such violence could flourish.

The real criminals were not just me, but the architects of the system that created the conditions for my actions, the policymakers who turned a blind eye to suffering, the wealthy who accumulated wealth at the expense of others, the individuals who chose comfort and privilege over empathy and social responsibility.

The justice system, in its supposed pursuit of truth and fairness, ignored the truth of my motivations, the underlying currents of societal dysfunction that fed my actions. It failed to recognize the invisible wounds, the deep-seated pain, the pervasive sense of injustice that had driven me to such extremes. It focused on the symptoms, ignoring the disease.

The failure of justice extended beyond my trial, reaching into the lives of every victim, every family impacted by my actions, every individual touched by the pervasive sense of insecurity and uncertainty that my actions had created. The fear, the pain, the sense of loss—these were the enduring legacies of the system's failure to address the root causes of crime.

The system sought to find closure in my incarceration. They could lock me away, but they couldn’t erase the scars, they couldn't bring back the dead, they couldn't heal the invisible wounds.

The silence in the courtroom, after the sentence was pronounced, was deafening, a heavy weight that hung in the air. It was a stark testament to the failure of justice, the failure to understand, the failure to heal. The system had delivered its punishment, a superficial sense of closure, but the deeper wounds remained, festering, invisible yet ever-present.

My sense of justice was twisted, warped, but it stemmed from a place of profound frustration, a deep sense of powerlessness in the face of systemic injustice. The system had failed its citizens, had neglected the invisible wounds that festered beneath the surface of society, and had enabled the conditions that allowed my actions to occur.

The system did not offer redress; it offered a sterile, emotionless pretense of justice, a punishment that could never truly atone for the devastating consequences of my acts. The unspoken truth, the invisible wounds, remained.

The trial was only the beginning, though. It was the spark, the ignition of something much larger. The city had to face what I had done, whether or not they liked it. As the trial unfolded, people started asking questions they had long ignored. The activists shouted louder, their voices amplified by my actions. The politicians, once comfortably insulated from the struggles of the city's poor, began scrambling to show they cared. They started talking about reform, about addressing inequality. But it was all too little, too late. They had built this system, and now they were reaping what they'd sown.

The elite, too, could no longer pretend to be untouchable. They scrambled, hiding behind new policies and charity initiatives, trying to absolve themselves of the guilt they felt creeping in. Some of them were terrified. They feared that the truth would come out—that they had been the silent architects of this chaos. Their wealth and power, once symbols of success, were now seen for what they truly were: symbols of oppression.

The fear spread like wildfire. The streets felt different. People no longer looked at their city the same way. The sense of invincibility that had defined the rich, the powerful, crumbled. They could feel their security slipping away, just as I had felt mine when I was one of them—entrenched in that world of privilege and indifference. They could see their own vulnerability, and it terrified them. Their illusion of control shattered.

But the real shift occurred in the hearts and minds of those long silenced—the forgotten, the neglected. My actions had given them a voice, though it came at a steep price. They saw me not as a villain, but as a mirror. I had forced the city to look at its own face and confront what it had hidden for so long. And in that reflection, they saw their own shame.

They locked me away, yes. They tried to forget. But the truth, the invisible wounds, would never go away. The city had been broken long before I made my move. And now, it would never be the same again. The proper punishment wasn't the prison sentence they handed me—it was the realization that the system that had allowed me to do what I did would never change unless they faced it head-on. And they never would. Not truly.

49

The fluorescent hum of the prison lights mocked the darkness that clung to me, a shadow cast by a past I couldn't outrun. They called it childhood trauma, a neat clinical term for the gaping maw of neglect that had swallowed my youth whole.

My parents, figures of icy indifference, rarely acknowledged my existence except to administer punishment or flaunt me to their elite friends. A misplaced teacup, a whispered word out of turn—these were crimes punishable by silence, by the chilling absence of warmth and affection. Their disapproval hung heavier than any physical blow. The house was a mausoleum of echoing emptiness, where silence screamed louder than any shout.

My earliest memories are fragmented, glimpses through a frosted glass: the hollow ache in my stomach, the constant chill seeping into my bones, the overwhelming loneliness that clung to me like a second skin. I learned early to become invisible, to shrink myself, to become a ghost in my own home. I existed only in the negative space, defined by what I lacked: love, attention, basic human decency.

The world outside, glimpsed through the grime-streaked windowpanes, seemed vibrant and full of life, a stark contrast to the barren landscape of my interior. It was a world I desperately longed to inhabit, a world that seemed forever out of reach.

The school was no sanctuary. I was a quiet, withdrawn child, an easy target for bullies. The taunts, the shoves, the callous disregard for my feelings—these became a part of the fabric of my existence, a brutal education in the cruelty of human nature.

I learned to expect pain, to brace myself for the inevitable onslaught of emotional and sometimes physical abuse. I retreated further into myself, building walls around my heart, constructing a fortress against the pain.

Then came the whispers, the hushed conversations behind cupped hands, the furtive glances that followed me like shadows. I was different; they said. Odd. Strange. The whispers became a constant hum, a background noise that permeated every aspect of my life. They were right, of course. I was different. I was damaged. I was broken.

I found solace in books, in the worlds created within the pages of novels and psychological thrillers. They became my escape, my refuge from the harsh realities of my life. Within the pages, I discovered the power of the human mind, the intricate mechanisms of the psyche, the ways in which trauma could shape and mold a personality.

I devoured books on criminology and psychology, fascinated by the twisted motivations that drove individuals to commit terrible acts. It was an exploration not of justification but of understanding. A dark, compelling exploration into the recesses of the human mind.

The characters I encountered in these books became my companions, their struggles to mirror my own in twisted ways. I identified with the villains, the outcasts, the misunderstood individuals who operated outside the bounds of societal norms. Their motivations, however warped, seemed more understandable than the cruelty and indifference of my reality.

As I grew older, the isolation deepened. The invisible wounds, once mere scratches on my soul, grew into festering sores, consuming my being. An emotional void ached within me, left empty by the lack of connection, yearning to be filled and soothed. The world, I discovered, is not a fair place. The powerful prey on the weak on this battlefield, thriving at the vulnerable's expense. My experience had taught me this lesson in the harshest possible way.

The resentment festered, a malignant growth, twisting my perception of reality, distorting my sense of justice. The system had failed me, had offered no protection, had provided no solace. I saw injustice everywhere I looked, a pervasive cancer eating away at the fabric of society. My anger became a potent force, a driving engine fueling my actions.

My actions were not born from a desire to inflict pain, although pain was certainly a byproduct. They were born from a place of profound frustration, a desperate yearning for justice, a twisted attempt to reclaim control in a world that had stripped me of it.

The game I played with Detective Stone was not just a game of hide-and-seek, but a reflection of my internal struggles, a desperate attempt to communicate the depth of my pain, the enormity of the invisible wounds that had shaped my life. His unwavering pursuit, his relentless investigation, mirrored my own internal battle.

Stone was a reflection of the relentless justice I sought, a justice that had always been denied me. He represented a system that, while flawed, represented an attempt at order in a chaotic world. He, in his own way, represented hope—hope my life had systematically eroded, yet it still flickered faintly, a beacon in the overwhelming darkness.

The courtroom, the trial, the eventual verdict—these were all mere stages in a much larger, more complex drama. By trying to punish me, the system failed to address the underlying issues causing my actions. The invisible wounds remained, festering beneath the surface, a constant reminder that true justice is far more elusive than the superficial sense of closure offered by the legal system.

My actions were a symptom, a desperate cry for help, a protest against a system that had utterly failed to address the underlying issues of societal injustice. The system had not only failed to protect me, but had enabled the conditions for my descent into darkness.

My story is a cautionary tale, a testament to the profound and lasting impact of trauma, a stark reminder that the wounds inflicted in childhood can shape a life in ways that are both unpredictable and devastating.

The unseen enemy is not just the darkness within us, but the pervasive indifference and systemic inequalities that create the fertile ground for it to flourish. The actual crime was not my actions, but the world that had created me.

50

The silence, I realize now, was the most insidious weapon. It wasn't the absence of sound, but the active suppression of truth, the deliberate smothering of the voice. My parents, masters of this insidious art, used silence as a form of control, a subtle yet brutal instrument of power. A wrong word, a misplaced object, a flicker of emotion—any deviation from their meticulously crafted image of perfection was met not with a scream or a slap, but with the chilling weight of silence, a suffocating blanket that smothered any expression of individuality. It was in those silences that fear bloomed, that the seed of resentment was sown, that the monster within me took root.

It wasn't just their silence, of course. It was the silence of the others, the neighbors who looked away, the teachers who dismissed my quiet pleas for help, the friends who stood by and watched as I was systematically eroded. The world observed my slow disintegration, my descent into darkness, and remained silent, complicit in my suffering.

Their silence was a tacit endorsement, a passive acceptance of the injustice I endured. It was a chilling lesson in the power of collective inaction, a horrifying demonstration of how easily a community can turn its back on the vulnerable.

This silence, this collective unwillingness to confront the darkness, this tacit acceptance of inequality—this was the root of the anger that festered within me. It wasn't born from a single event, a singular trauma, but from a slow accumulation of injustices, a steady drip-drip-drip of emotional neglect and societal apathy.

The world, I discovered, is not a fair place. Justice, as it is conventionally understood, is a myth. It is a comforting delusion that masks the brutal reality of power dynamics. The privileged thrive, insulated by layers of protection, while the vulnerable are tossed aside, their cries for help lost in the deafening silence of indifference.

Stone represented a different silence—the silence of the system, the silent weight of the law. He was a dedicated professional, yet his investigation also served as a painful reminder of the limits of justice. He was the embodiment of the institutional indifference I sought to expose, a symbol of a system that failed to prevent the violence, a system that, despite its best efforts, couldn't truly grasp the root causes of my actions.

It wasn't a game, not in the way that he, or society at large, perceived it. It was a desperate cry for help, a scream into the void. The murders were a dramatic monologue played out on the stage of society. Each victim represented a specific facet of the injustice that had shaped my existence, each death a carefully placed punctuation mark in a long, unspoken sentence.

The silence surrounding these acts, the hesitant whispers, the hushed conversations—they fueled my actions. The more the world remained silent, the louder my actions became, a grotesque counterpoint to the pervasive apathy.

It was a perverse form of communication; a desperate

attempt to break through the barrier of collective denial and force the world to acknowledge the long-ignored pain and suffering.

The price of silence is high, far higher than anyone can imagine. It's a price measured not in years or punishment, but in the erosion of hope, the extinguishing of faith, the slow, insidious decay of the human spirit. It is the slow, agonizing death of the soul, a silent scream swallowed by the indifference of the world. In its silence, the world permitted the monster to grow, fester, and bloom within me until it was uncontainable.

The price of silence is not just borne by the victim, but by everyone who remains silent. It’s a collective responsibility, a shared burden, a stain that contaminates the collective consciousness. The silence complicates the search for truth; it shields the perpetrators, and it perpetuates the cycle of violence.

The silence of the bystanders, the silence of the authorities, the silence of society—it all contributed to the creation of the monster I became. It was not my creation alone; it was a collective creation, a grotesque offspring born of apathy and inaction.

And what of my own silence? The calculated silence I employed, the controlled words I chose to whisper in the ears of the reader? That, too, was a part of the game. The manipulation, the control, the subtle implicating of the reader —these were all part of the performance, a complex psychological manipulation designed to expose the innate fascination with the dark side, the hidden complicity within the observer.

The truth is not a simple narrative of good versus evil, but a tangled web of causation and effect, a labyrinthine exploration of human nature at its most broken and beautiful. The story is not just my story, it's the story of a world that failed to speak out, a world that allowed the darkness to thrive in silence. It is a story meant to awaken, expose, and provoke. A story to break the silence, pierce the veil of complacency, and force a confrontation with the brutal truth that lies beneath the surface.

It is a story about the price of silence, a price we all pay. The question is, are we willing to pay for it anymore? Are we willing to break the silence? Or will we continue to watch, silently, as the monsters rise? The choice, as always, is yours.

51

The facade of my life, the murders—all of it was a performance, a desperate attempt to break the suffocating silence that had enveloped me since childhood. Stone, with his dogged pursuit, was merely another actor in this grand, tragic play. He represented the system, the law, the very structure that had failed to protect me, that had allowed the monster within to flourish. In a twisted way, he served as a necessary component of my narrative, a foil against which my actions could be defined.

The connections, the seemingly random threads that Stone painstakingly weaved together, revealed more about the systemic failures than about my individual pathology. Each victim, a carefully selected symbol of the privileged class, highlighted the gaping chasm between the haves and the have-nots, the brutal indifference of a society that valued comfort and wealth over empathy and justice.

There was a certain irony, of course, in my chosen victims. They were not inherently evil, not monsters in the way I had become. They were simply complicit, beneficiaries of a system that allowed such grotesque inequalities to flourish. Their obliviousness, their comfortable distance from the suffering of the less fortunate, made them perfect symbols of the silent complicity that fueled my rage.

The last victim, however, was different. They are not a member of the elite, not a symbol of wealth and privilege. They are a reflection of the systemic failure to protect the vulnerable, a casualty of a society that prioritized the appearance of order over genuine justice.

Their death was not a calculated move, not a carefully orchestrated performance, but a spontaneous eruption, an uncontrolled outburst of years of repressed rage and accumulated pain. They represented the shattering of my meticulously constructed narrative, the crumbling of the carefully crafted facade I had created.

The ending, therefore, is not a neat resolution, not a tidy conclusion. It's an unraveling, a disintegration of the narrative itself, mirroring the disintegration of my sanity. The game, as Stone perceived it, ended with my capture. But for me, the game never really ended. It continues, it strengthens, it transforms, adapting to the changing circumstances. The silence, however, is broken. My silence, at least, is shattered.

The reader, I realize now, has been a crucial player in this entire performance. My confession, my narrative, my direct address—these were all carefully crafted strategies designed to engage you, to provoke a reaction, to implicate you in the dark drama that unfolded. Your fascination, your morbid curiosity, your complicity in my twisted game—these are all part of the larger narrative, a testament to the allure of the forbidden, the attraction to the dark side of human nature.

The unanswered questions, the loose ends, the lingering uncertainties—these are not mere flaws in the narrative, but essential elements of the design. They leave you suspended, questioning, questioning your own reactions, your own complicity. They challenge your assumptions, your preconceived notions of justice, of morality, of human nature. The truth, as I have shown you, is rarely neat, rarely tidy. It is messy, complicated, disturbing, and profoundly unsettling.

The silence surrounding these acts, the societal reluctance to confront the darkness within us, the avoidance of hard truths—this is the true villain of this story. It's the collective silence, the passive acceptance of injustice, the unwillingness to challenge the status quo that allows monsters like me to flourish. It's the silent complicity that fuels the cycle of violence, the apathy that allows suffering to continue unchecked.

I am not seeking absolution, nor am I offering excuses. I am merely laying bare the truth, a truth that is both terrifying and liberating. The truth is, the monster I became was not solely my creation. A world unwilling to confront its own darkness nurtured, nourished, and gave life to the monster. It was a monster born not just of my personal suffering, but of the systemic injustices, the societal apathy, the deafening silence that permeated the world I inhabited.

The price of silence, as I have discovered, is high. It's a price measured not in years of incarceration, not in the legal penalties imposed upon the perpetrator, but in the erosion of hope, the decay of the soul, the slow, agonizing death of the human spirit. It's a price paid by victims and perpetrators alike, a price shared by those who remain silent, complicit in the cycle's perpetuation of violence.

My hope, in revealing this narrative, this twisted confession, is to break the silence, to force a confrontation with the darkness that lurks within us all. To show that the monsters we fear are often born not of inherent evil, but of neglect, of apathy, of the silent complicity of those who choose to turn away. It is a story meant not to justify but to expose, not to excuse but to challenge, not to condemn but to awaken.

The questions remain. Will the world learn from this? Will we break the silence, or will our continued silence perpetuate the cycle of violence and allow the next monster to rise from the ashes of apathy and indifference? The answer, as always, lies not with me, but with you. The choice, my reader, is yours.

The last victim is coming, and the game is yours to play.

52

Remember when I told you the rose was a symbol? That it wasn't just an innocent gift, but something far more sinister? I wasn't lying. I never lie. Not to you. Lies are for fools and the weak-willed. The truth is always more powerful, more intoxicating, more damning.

And here you are, still reading, still clinging to the words like a lifeline. But let me ask you something—have you even considered what happens next? Have you stopped to question what I've been leading you toward? Or are you simply too enthralled, too seduced by the story to realize you've already lost yourself to it?

Detective Stone would tell you he's the hero. That he's the one who will uncover the truth, bring justice, and close this chapter once and for all. He believes in that tired old trope—the relentless detective and the monster he pursues. But what if I told you he was never the one holding the pen? What if I told you the ending was never his to write?

Stone found the rose, of course. He traced its origins, followed by the breadcrumbs I so generously left behind. He combed through my past, my victims, the carefully orchestrated chaos I'd left in my wake. And he thought—oh, how he thought—that he was closing in. That he was winning.

But the truth? The truth is far more delicious.

I let him find me. The grand revelation, the final confrontation, the moment of supposed triumph—handed to him on a silver platter. He wanted justice, but justice is a construct, a fairytale told to keep society from unraveling. What he got instead was doubt. A crack in his perfectly structured world. The doubt that festers, that gnaws at the soul, that whispers in the dark when sleep refuses to come.

Stone arrested me. He walked me out in cuffs, a victorious gleam in his tired eyes. The world watched, the headlines screamed, the city exhaled in collective relief. The killer was caught. The nightmare was over. Except… was it?

You see, the beauty of a well-crafted narrative is that it lingers. Even after you turn the last page, after the credits roll, after the curtain falls, it lingers. It lingers in the mind, in the whispers exchanged in hushed voices, in the way shadows seem just a little too long, too dark. In the way people hesitate before accepting a gift—a rose, perhaps.

They put me in a cell. They surrounded me with concrete and steel, thinking that would be enough. But what is a cage to someone like me? What are bars to a mind that has already escaped? I have new friends now—women with their own stories, their own traumas, their own darkness. They sit with me in book club, in therapy, in the yard beneath the sun that never quite warms. They listen. They learn.

And then there's you.

You think you are merely an observer, safe within the confines of your home, turning the pages, indulging in a harmless fascination. But that's the illusion I've let you believe. You were never just reading. You were participating. Every turn of the page, every pause as your breath hitched, every flicker of fear in your mind—I have seen it. I have felt it. You have been my subject all along.

The final victim, unlike the others, wasn't a symbol of societal excess, a representation of the gilded cage they inhabited. This victim is different. This victim is… you.

Not you, physically, of course. That would be far too clumsy, too obvious. No, the final victim is the reflection of you within me, the part of you that is drawn to darkness, that finds a twisted fascination in the eerie. The part of you that sits here, reading this, engrossed in the narrative of my depravity.

This is not a dramatic confrontation, a thrilling chase, or a violent showdown. This is the gradual realization of your own complicity. The insidious creep of doubt, the unraveling of your understanding of reality, the chilling realization that you are not merely an observer, but a participant in a grand, terrifying game of psychological manipulation.

You, who have followed me to this moment. You, who have devoured my words, let them seep into your thoughts, curl around your subconscious like a serpent coiling tighter and tighter. You, who sit in your safe little world, believing the walls around you will keep you separate from me.

You see, I have always been fascinated by the human psyche. I understand its complexities, its vulnerabilities, its inherent capacity for both great compassion and chilling cruelty. The others, my previous victims, were merely illustrations of my theories, examples of societal decay. You, however, represent something far more profound. You represent the darker aspects of humanity, the parts we try to ignore, the fascination we have with the forbidden.

The murder wasn't a physical act, not in the traditional

sense. It was a slow, insidious process, a carefully orchestrated dismantling of your perceptions, a meticulous unraveling of your sanity. It began with the rose, a symbol of beauty used as a weapon of psychological warfare. It continued with the gradual revelation of truths, carefully masked as fiction. Every word, every carefully crafted sentence, was a blade, slicing through your defenses.

And you let it happen. You welcomed it. Page after page, you let me in. You let me whisper in your ear, let me pull you closer, let me make you doubt the very walls around you. You thought you could stop at any time. You thought you were in control. But tell me, if you're in control, why can't you put the book down? Why do you keep reading?

Do you feel it? That creeping unease? That doubt slipping under your skin? You read about the others and thought yourself different. Thought you were only an observer. But I've told you from the beginning—you were never just watching. You were participating. The act of reading, of consuming, of imagining—do you understand the power of that? Do you grasp what it means to step willingly into my world?

I may be behind bars, but I am not contained. Not really. Because I am here. In your mind. In the stories you tell yourself, in the memories you can't quite trust anymore, in the way you hesitate before turning off the light at night.

And what of Detective Stone? What of the man who chased shadows only to find them staring back? He will go on, of course. That is his role. He will stand before cameras, say the right things, let the world believe in closure. But in the quiet, when no one is watching, he will wonder. He will remember the look in my eyes as he locked me away. He will question if justice was ever truly served or if he was merely another pawn, moving exactly as I intended.

And society? They will celebrate my capture, tell themselves the danger has passed. But fear lingers. It festers. They will look over their shoulders, suspect their neighbors, hesitate before accepting a stranger's kindness. And every time they see a crimson rose, they will wonder.

The story never truly ends. Not for them. Not for Stone. Not for you.

Because I am still here. And you are still reading.

So tell me…

Are you sure you're alone?